D0064977

Tender Romance™ is proud to present
a double bill

Two brand-new short stories
in one volume…

Firstly international bestselling author

PENNY JORDAN

makes a guest appearance
in Tender Romance™

Penny Jordan is best known for her
intense, passionate Modern Romance™
novels. MY SECRET WISH LIST has
just as much sparkle, just the same
talent—but offering you a new type of
story. Written in a diary format, this
short story is fresh, flirty and feel-good!
Prepare yourself for something
completely different!

DARCY MAGUIRE

is a fresh, exciting new talent
in Tender Romance™.
A GIRL'S BEST FRIEND
is a lively, emotional story
full of colourful characters!

Enjoy!

Dear Reader,

We're constantly striving to bring you the best romance fiction by the most exciting authors, and in Tender Romance™ we're especially keen to feature fresh, sparkling, emotionally exhilarating novels! Modern love stories to suit your every mood: poignant, deeply moving stories; lively, upbeat romances with sparks flying; or sophisticated, edgy novels with a cosmopolitan flavour.

All our authors are special, and we hope you continue to enjoy each month's new selection of Tender Romances. This month we're delighted to feature two short stories in one volume, both of which come with extra fizz! Follow Kitty's hilarious antics in MY SECRET WISH LIST from Penny Jordan. (Expect something completely different from her Modern Romance™ stories!) Then dip in to Casey's chatty, fun & fast-paced diary—from new Tender Romance™ talent Darcy Macguire!

We hope you enjoy **WHAT WOMEN WANT!**— it's fresh, flirty and feel-good!—and look out for future sparkling stories in Tender Romance™. If you'd like to share your thoughts and comments with us, do please write to:

The Tender Romance Editors
Harlequin Mills & Boon Ltd
Eton House, 18-24 Paradise Road
Richmond, Surrey TW9 1SR
Or e-mail us at: tango@hmb.co.uk

Happy reading!

The Editors

WHAT WOMEN WANT!

PENNY JORDAN
&
DARCY MAGUIRE

MILLS & BOON®

First published in Great Britain 2002
Large Print edition 2003
Harlequin Mills & Boon Limited,
Eton House, 18-24 Paradise Road,
Richmond, Surrey TW9 1SR

WHAT WOMEN WANT!
© HARLEQUIN ENTERPRISES II B.V. 2002

MY SECRET WISH LIST © Penny Jordan 2002
A GIRL'S BEST FRIEND © Darcy Maguire 2002

ISBN 0 263 17903 6

Set in Times Roman 15¼ on 16¼ pt.
16-0503-56387

Printed and bound in Great Britain
by Antony Rowe Ltd, Chippenham, Wiltshire

MY SECRET WISH LIST

by
PENNY JORDAN

Born in Preston, Lancashire, **Penny Jordan** now lives in a beautiful fourteenth-century house in rural Cheshire. Penny has been writing for over ten years and now has over one hundred novels to her name, including the phenomenally successful POWER PLAY and SILVER. With over thirty million copies of her books in print, and translations into seventeen languages, she has firmly established herself as a novelist of great scope.

Look out for more Penny Jordan books, coming soon in Modern Romance™.

CHAPTER ONE

THIS is it, then, is it? This is all I've got to show for my life. Apart from droopy boobs. This is what it all comes down to. Me, the computer, and a medical diagnosis that says that I must stop being self-pitying and accept that I am past sell-by-date! I must conquer unattractive and immature desire to possess Madonna-style bod and a stomach washboard-flat enough to flaunt navel stud.

That's one of the reasons I am keeping this diary. As a form of therapy. On the advice of the personal, one-to-one life-changing session I had with one of the universe's top life-coaches (a birthday present from trendy stepsister who works in Public Relations—well, it was more of a consolation present, really.) The one-to-one session was a ten-minute phone call and an impossible-to-fill-in questionnaire which came in the post and which I thought was junk mail. Luckily managed to rescue it from the rubbish before Mr Russell—that's the elderly pensioner who lives two doors down— dumped his dog's poop-a-scoop in my wheelie bin.

Anyway, one of the things life-coach instructed me to do was keep a diary, so that I could write down all thoughts and feelings and thus find out

hidden meaning behind own self-destructive ten-
dencies—like eating chocolates and agonising over
non-husband's opinion that boobs are saggy when
I should be going to gym and should also be doing
helpful things in community, like busybody neighbour from three up who patrols local park counting
number of discarded used condoms.

I have always been a sucker for a bit of self-
indulgence, which is probably why I am currently
two stone overweight—well, actually it's only one
stone ten pounds now, but scales haven't been re-
liable ever since they were used under broken leg
of late mother-in-law's commode.

So here I am, aged fifty-one, miserable, moody
and menopausal.

Hard to believe that five weeks ago I was con-
gratulating myself on how serene, successful and
satisfying own life was. But that was before
daughter sent me a birthday card which read
'Happy Easter'; son rang from university to say he
was putting off taking his finals because he wanted
to 'chill out' for a year or two first. Oh and—
almost forgot—before my husband came home too
late to take me out for the celebratory dinner I'd
booked at Chez Luigi's (Luigi is Italian, but Roux
Brothers-trained, and he's very good about Derek
only ordering one starter and one sweet, asking for
two sets of cutlery and then complaining about the
small portions).

I was in bed, eating the last of the Christmas chocolates—the soft cream centres which I really hate and always leave until I am *really* desperate—wrapped in typical husbandly Christmas present of flannelette nightdress big enough to go round myself twice. Husband had written tender little note with the present, saying he thought it would be large enough to hide gross sight of droopy boobs.

(Husband has definitely got 'from Mars' sense of humour and thought it very funny to send self birthday card showing hideous old hag lifting skirt to reveal boobs down to knees, having written inside that the card reminded him of me.)

Anyway, husband walked in wearing oversize shiny nylon trousers that he thinks make him look trendy but in reality make him look like a chimpanzee. I suppose it's not husband's fault, though, that he has short legs and big stomach.

Husband's earlobe was still weeping from the new earring he had put in. His tattoo was finally scabbing over and his hair finally beginning to grow again after Beckham haircut that went wrong. Husband said he'd got something to tell me. Thought it was going to be a joke. Well, in a way it was.

He said that we didn't have anything in common any more. This is a complete lie. What about our huge mortgage and the set of semi-antique chairs his mother gave us, two with wonky legs, and one with 'Digger loves Jimmy' scratched on it? (Jimmy was his uncle. He never married.) Not to mention the twenty-seven years of marriage and the two children we produced?

But what do twenty-seven years of unwanted memories and two children mean to a man who's head over heels in lust with a raving nymphomaniac of a twenty-something-year-old woman called Cheree (it was Sheryl, but she changed it) with dyed blonde hair and enormous inflated breasts?

My own best friend, Jacki (who knocked the 'e' off the end at the same time as she 'lost' years off her age and 'found' herself in the Gambia with some toyboy who made her realise what life was really all about), says I could have boobs lifted, but I can't see the point since no one else but me is ever going to see them again. Luckily my own eyesight isn't what it was!

Jacki's divorced now. She loves it. She got to keep the house, the car, and David's money! But I think that must have had something to do with the affair she was having with their accountant.

Derek—that's my own husband—well, *was* my husband—is now rushing through the divorce because he doesn't want to leave any messy ends when he and Cheree leave the country and she's concerned that if he dies whilst they're away I will inherit everything. (She must mean all his debts, because Derek swears there isn't any money).

Derek told me that he and Cheree were going to
sail round the world together and that he'd already
sold the business—that alone was a shock 'cos
only the previous week he'd been moaning that the
business was losing so much money he'd be lucky
to give it away!

And the money it was losing wasn't really
ours—not strictly speaking! It was the money the
building society had given us and in exchange we
had given them the deeds to our previously almost-
paid-for house—the only asset we had apart from
the pension which Derek cashed in early to put into
the business.

Derek was originally a salesman but then had
brainwave to set up own business as a 'Disenfran-
chised Refrigeration Unit Relocation and
Rehabilitation Consultant'. No, I haven't a clue
what it means either—but it must have something
to do with old fridges since our garage was full of
them until they got taken away at dead of night.

I just hope that husband remembers to tell
Cheree to pack his anti-seasickness tablets—he
was once terribly ill on the channel ferry. It was
just as well that the ferry hadn't actually left the
harbour at the time, because if it had heaven knows
what might have happened. It was a bit embarrassing when they had to unload all the cars because ours was first on. We'd missed the earlier
ferry because Derek hadn't tied the luggage rack

on roof securely enough. The cases had fallen off, and so we'd had to wait for the next one. Anyway, I am sure Derek was being unfair when he said that those dents in the car were put there deliberately by other happy holidaymakers.

Of course Cheree won't have much to pack. For a start she only wears bikini bottoms and not tops, on account of fabric rubbing on her very sensitive nipples. (Husband told me about her little problem—well, not so little, really. He told me last year, when he took her to a conference in Brighton, and I saw them both on television lying on the beach. Apparently that was why he'd been rubbing cream into her nipples. He didn't want her suing him for employer negligence on health grounds.)

I suppose I knew then, really, but I told myself it was just a phase he was going through and that we were both too adult and sensible to throw away a marriage as solid as ours. Jacki said at the time that it was no wonder Cheree had had her boobs inflated. At least now they stuck out as far as her teeth.

For the first week after Derek told me THE NEWS I didn't do anything. Well, there wasn't anything I could do, really. And then the estate agent arrived and said that the house should sell pretty easily but that it was a pity it wasn't in better decorative order. No one wants plum-coloured bathroom suites any more. I told Derek that when we bought them.

We were doing up this large Victorian house we'd bought for a song—well, not so much a song as a whole opera—when we found out about rotten floorboards and roof timbers. He said the plum bathroom suites were a bargain and wouldn't show the dirt. His mother said he was probably thinking about his grandparents. Apparently they kept coal in their bath!

But then the estate agent mentioned his fees, and Derek blew a fuse and said he would sell house himself. Why pay greedy, unprincipled rogue of agent when an up-market, lovingly restored des-res like ours, in a prestigious part of town, would have people queuing up to take it off our hands?

Agent pointed out that by law you're not allowed now to lie about property. Derek went red in the face and said it hadn't stopped them when we had bought the house through the same estate agency. Agent stopped him to ask if had eradicated all woodworm and replaced floorboards.

After agent had gone, Derek said I should never have admitted that we had not, and that he couldn't afford to have the asking price reduced by £50,000. He said that I was deliberately trying to make things difficult for him and was behaving like total cow, just as Cheree had said I would.

Anyway, agent left after Derek refused to sign form declaring no problems with neighbours! He couldn't sign it, really—not when whole street knows that family five down is so incensed with Derek parking his old banger—sorry, company car—outside their house so that he wouldn't lower the tone of our house that they took all wheels off the car one night and put it up on bricks. They would have had it towed away, but scrap dealer didn't want it!

Our house now has homemade 'For Sale' sign leaning drunkenly in front garden, but so far there haven't been any viewers apart from man from council wanting to know if Derek has planning permission for searchlight he put up outside to deter would-be thieves (and the tomcat from next door).

Of course I had to ring Derek to tell him about son's plans. Obviously Derek has more fatherly concern than previously evident as he came straight round! His mobile rang when he arrived—it plays the opening bars of 'We are Sailing'.

Derek said son was old enough to make his own decisions and that he couldn't afford to keep him at university any longer anyway. Derek also asked if anyone had made an offer on the house. He said there should be enough equity in it after we've paid off the mortgage for me to buy myself a little flat—apparently property's v. cheap in certain parts of country and no need really for me to greedily take up so much space in such an expensive part. Also pointed out that if I had got a job all those years ago, when he asked me to, I would be in a much better position today to take care of myself financially. I didn't know just what a strain he had found it supporting me.

Cheree earns a very good salary, he added.

Since he employs her, I suppose he must be right. However, I did remind him that the reason I could not work was that I took care of his incontinent, infirm mother for ten years.

Husband replied that at least Mother had pension, and also money from sale of her own house, to contribute to the household.

Felt like reminding him that his mother gambled away all her pension playing bingo until she was banned from local old folks' club for almost causing an affair—yes, we thought she'd made a mistake at first, and it should have been affray, but turned out she was right. She had tried to steal husband off another woman. Mother-in-law claimed hadn't tried to steal at all, but had won so much from other woman that she had been forced to put up husband as collateral.

Husband said we needed to make sure we get a quick sale because he and Cheree wanted to spend the winter in the Caribbean—and besides, the building society were pressing for overdue mortgage payments. Husband also v. kindly said he had decided to put house in my name—if I would just sign form agreeing to hand over any equity in sale to him. Said I would think about it.

CHAPTER TWO

SPENT second week sorting out the contents of the attic, in between bouts of tears and eating chocolate.

That was when stepsister rang. We've always had challenging relationship with one another. After all, her mother pinched my father from my mother... She got to live with them whilst I had to stay with my mother—who, not having my father to embrace any longer, embraced religion instead. Well, if you call witches' spells and naked dancing round bonfires religion.

Tara, that's my stepsister, was sent to St Hilda's Private School for Girls!

She had a gold watch for her thirteenth birthday and ice skates! My mother wanted to give me a toad, and a book on how to cast spells.

My mother was always ahead of her time. And it wasn't her fault that the local council refused to see the benefit of her plan to hold parties to recruit new witches. They said that all the naked dancing was causing a nuisance and that people were complaining. And anyway, it was a definite health hazard on account of bare feet touching uncleansed ground of local park. Mother did an interview for

17

local paper, but due to confusion at printers, the interview was printed under name of local v. moral councillor. Councillor was totally outraged when my mother was elected in her place.

Now Mum lives in California, with her fourth husband. I don't hear from her very much.

Derek never really approved of her. His own parents were very traditional and old-fashioned. We only found out about his father liking to dress up in women's clothes after he died. He had written in his will that the wanted to be buried in his favourite evening dress. Of course Derek's mother pretended that it was just a joke, and in the end he was buried in his suit.

Anyway, Tara has her own PR company. She's never married. For every decade she's past she's had another piece of plastic surgery—which is why at fifty she looks thirty, but in a tight, shiny, this-skin-is-killing-me sort of way.

Still, like I said, she caught me at a bad moment. I'd just found the box containing our wedding photographs and cards from Derek which I'd kept!

Had forgotten I was once so sentimental and optimistic! Found the one he sent me when we got engaged, with a rude poem in it which he'd promised to put into practice. Well, it wasn't his fault that the rugby team decided to walk home down lovers' lane that night. And at least they had the decency to lift the car back onto the road again afterwards.

It was a bit embarrassing, though, because the car belonged to his father, and the next day, when he went to pick up his boss from the station, Derek's father opened the glove compartment to give his boss a tissue and handed him my knickers by mistake.

Of course we had to get married after that. Well, you did in those days, didn't you?

It was the seventies. The sexual revolution might have overwhelmed the moral barricades of the mothers of London's teenagers. But for us 'oop North', believe you me, Victorian ethics still ruled!

Anyway, back to my stepsister's phone call this week. There I was sobbing, feeling all emotional and crying into the special-price low-fat vanilla ice-cream that was all I could find in the freezer to come anywhere close to self indulgence, when the phone rang. Of course I had to tell her what had happened!

Straight away she said she knew just the thing to get me back on track and turn my whole life around. She said that it had saved her sanity when she had been so stressed out about breaking her nails just before she had to collect the winning contestant from *Kidnapped* to take to TV Awards Ceremony!

(*Kidnapped* was a groundbreaking new TV programme where a specially chosen group of contestants had to go out and kidnap someone and the
viewers had to give them marks on how real they
made it. This contestant had done so well that the
person being kidnapped had a heart attack from
shock on screen and had to be resuscitated by ac-
tors from the accident and emergency soap in next
studio.)

Tara said she would 'treat me', because this life-
coach was just so in demand she charged the earth
and that usually she wouldn't be seen dead coaching anyone who wasn't someone…

I wasn't sure.

I mean, a life-coach…just what does that mean?

Jacki and my other friend Rosie were well impressed when I told them!

Jacki did say, though, that she thought I'd have
got more benefit from a night with a sexy stud
escort!

One of her friends had been given one as a surprise fortieth birthday present by her girlfriends.
And then to make it really special they'd had the
whole thing videoed. Unfortunately, though,
there'd been some crossed wires, and the video had
got played at her fortieth birthday party. Her husband said that with a backside like hers she should
have been ashamed to have it publicly displayed
like that.

Anyway, she's divorced now, and she's running an agency that finds out if your husband is likely to be unfaithful by getting some stunning-looking girl to try to seduce him. So far the score is Stunning-looking Girls l00, Husbands 0! Surprise. Surprise.

So the life-coach rang the afternoon I'd just spent comfort-reading my old Georgette Heyer books. Where, oh, where are the Heyer men right now when I could do with one? Dangerous, passionate. And desperately determined to ravish me. That would show Derek!

Okay, okay, I know. That is so shallow. But then I am shallow!

Speaking of sexy, gorgeous-looking men, I have just seen the new owner of house at end of street. The house the poshest in the area—huge garden, detached and completely refurbished by local interior designer who once appeared on TV designer programme.

Her clients, the previous owners, complained that they hated what she'd done and that they couldn't understand how undyed calico curtains for their drawing room could possibly have cost £5,000 when anyone could buy the same fabric down the market for 30p a metre! It was all sorted out amicably in end, when designer explained that their calico was special import and totally exclusive 'cos was made in a unique way.

Never liked to tell neighbour that I had seen the labels from the bales of cloth delivered when they were away and Derek went scavenging in their skip. (Derek said it was totally neighbourly act since he was concerned that their builders might try to remove and sell on irreplaceable period features, such as the Victorian fireplace he bought off them for a mere £500.) Label on cloth said quite definitely that fabric was from Pakistan and 10p per metre.

Derek never said anything. Well, he was in shock for months afterwards once he discovered that the builder was flogging fireplaces just like ours at a local car boot sale for £50.

Anyway, trendy couple who owned house have gone to live on remote island where will be no contamination from modern living. (Actually, have heard that truth is he lost his job and child has been expelled from school for knowing more than teacher.)

New owner was getting out of sleek, expensive-looking black car when he walked past this morning. Furniture van was pulling up outside.

Of course didn't want to make curiosity obvious, so just took a quick glance.

New neighbour is male—very much so—sexy broad shoulders, shown off in white tee shirt that revealed even sexier athletic-type flat stomach. Thick dark hair, just tinged with grey, gorgeous super-sexy silver-grey eyes and thick black eye-lashes!

In addition to immaculate white tee shirt he was wearing well-cut chinos and clean shoes—and *no* wedding ring! Not that I was paying too much attention. (Not much!) Had to put down bags of supermarket shopping which I was carrying 'cos Derek has taken car.

However, panicked when new neighbour saw me and started to walk over. In rush to get away unobtrusively I forgot how much I had pushed into flimsy plastic shopping bags. Served me right that pack of Vitamins for the Older Woman fell out right in front of him.

Quite proud of my quick recovery, though, when I claimed vitamins were for elderly friend!

Image spoiled when demon skateboarding sons of family from five down skated past and shouted, 'Move it, Grandma!'

Still, every cloud has a silver lining, and life-coach has said I must always look for positive in everything, so just as well that I was wrapped up against cold in face-muffling scarf and old coat!

Apparently you have to really work at this life-coaching stuff… Life-coach has given me all sorts of exercises to do. Like this one:

Imagine yourself in twenty years' time. Where do you want to be? Who do you want to be?

Twenty years' time! Will be seventy-one! OHMYGOD!

Immediately feel depressed and pervy for having spent rest of day fantasising about sexy new neighbour, mentally imagining him in Georgette Heyer hero mode, rescuing me from horrid wicked Sir Jasper type and clasping my delicate, fragile frame in strong male arms…

Anyway, I'd rather imagine myself twenty years ago… Two stone lighter, thicker hair, a belly like a supermodel's… So okay, maybe I am exaggerating slightly…

Let's see—in twenty years' time I want to be like Tina Turner! As she is now!

Think of ten things you want to achieve before you reach your next decade birthday!
Think challenging!! Exciting!!! Innovative!!!!

Oh, yeah! Like what?

In a fit of irritation, reach for notepad and start to write down most implausible things I can think of!

- Learn to inline skate
- Be swept off feet by hero strikingly similar to new sexy neighbour at No. 14, just like in Georgette Heyer's books!
- Be able to make melt-in-mouth pastry like smug busybody neighbour from three up

- Be able to look so sexy in quick-release thong and see-thru bra that no one cares about pastry!
- Learn to salsa
- Be picked as salsa partner by sexy new neighbour for very private one-to-one lessons
- Own bright red convertible with rude private number
- Discover sexy new neighbour is madly in love with self
- Discover boobs have miraculously undrooped
- Discover husband has secret prescription for Viagra and burn it!

I read list and find I have the number I need. Well, I think I will forget about pastry-making—and husband!

Look further down list of life-coach's bossy instructions:

And then think of ten more!
Then write down ten things you like about yourself!

Er…

Good sense of humour—even if Derek always complains that I never laugh at his jokes. Apparently Cheree laughs like a hyena at them—Jacki says that she looks like one as well!

Good friend—okay, so I didn't tell Rosie when my son said that Rosie's schoolteacher niece was giving boys at school hands-on sex education lessons. But how was I to know exactly what he meant? I was as shocked as everyone else when news broke in the papers that she had run away with twelve-year-old pupil she was supposed to be giving extra after-school coaching? Anyway, all the fuss has died down now, and Rosie's niece has moved to another part of the country. She's got a job there teaching at an all-boys boarding school.

I am a good mother.

Well, I have tried to be a good mother.

Not entirely all own fault that daughter has turned out so odd—probably takes after my mother, and therefore definitely not my fault.

Am an optimist—true. Look at the way am fantasising about new sexy neighbour!

Am good with money—well, I would be if I had any!

How many is that?

Could put down loads more good points, but am too selfless to want to bore on about own virtues!

Think what you would do if you won the lottery.

Would pay off enormous mortgage, for a start, and son's student loan. Might even have droopy boobs fixed after all.

Whilst I was thinking, Derek rang to say he'd

accepted an offer for the house. The only thing was there isn't going to be as much equity as he'd hoped—but the good news is that once all the expenses have been deducted (apparently he had forgotten about certain unpaid bills), there should still be enough for me to put down a deposit on a small flat. And after all I wouldn't need anything bigger than that, really. In fact small bedsit would suit admirably… Also v. generously said it would do me good to get a job, if I could get one, that is, at my advanced age!

I am trying to look for job. Rosie says new hypermarket is looking for shelf-packers and is favouring 'mature personnel' because they can read the labels on things and don't spend all day on their mobile phones texting messages that say things like 'RU there—txt me!'

But I would need a car to get there, since is out of town. Keep checking local paper for suitable work, and suitable flat, but so far haven't found anything.

CHAPTER THREE

STILL haven't completed first exercise for life-coach—i.e. supply list of 'goals'—but this morning have doctor's appointment to check how am doing with HRT.

Doctor's surgery full of usual dreadful examples of humanity at its worst—the receptionists—whilst poor unfortunate patients cower in dread of incurring their wrath.

I give my name and creep past to find a seat. My doctor is running forty minutes late with her appointments.

Pick up a magazine—a *Cosmopolitan* that's twelve months out of date. There's an article inside: 'Thirty things you should have done by the time you are thirty'. Start to read it.

1   Had sex in ten different positions
2   That do not appear in the *Kama Sutra*
3   With ten different men
4   Consecutively
5   Concurrently
6   Snogged your best friend's brother
7   Snogged your best friend's man
8   Snogged your best friend's father

9   Snogged your best friend
10   Got off a speeding fine by using feminine charms
11   Have on at least two occasions woken up in a strange bed unable to remember how you got there or with whom
12   Smoked a joint
13   Had sex in a public place
14   Ended a long-term relationship and discovered it was the best thing you ever did
15   Travelled round the world three times
16   Seduced a younger man
17   Told your mother that she could never be mistaken for your sister
18   Had a religious experience
19   Had a surreal experience
20   Spent twenty-four days scared to death you might be pregnant
21   Spent twenty-four hours crying because you weren't
22   Had sex at work whilst on phone to boss
23   Had sex with boss whilst on phone to partner or mother

Et cetera.
Realise miserably that have lived totally boring, unachieving life, since I haven't done any of them.
    Sneakily rip page out of mag. Good joke to show friends. Then realise that elderly woman next

to me is glaring disapprovingly and looks as though she is about to summon frightening head-mistress of a receptionist.

Relief is at hand. (There's an item about that too, but too rude for me to read.) Finally hear my name called.

My doctor looks like a TV presenter—all glowing skin, thick soft hair and a look in her eyes which says oh-God-not-another-dreary-middle-aged-might-have-been-but-wasn't.

Tell her my HRT has made me put on two stone. Has also failed to inflate boobs, as described in magazines by confident women MPs. Ask if she can explain mystery as to why for every two hairs that were on head I now only have one, whilst disgusting black wire has started growing on chin.

(Jacki says it could be worse—you can at least have extensions on head. She says too that Afro-Caribbean plaits work almost as well as a facelift at pulling skin tight.)

Doctor looks dubious. Starts to ask me about my diet and my sex life. I try to explain both are total non-starters, but she is already on computer providing repeat prescription. Tells me to think about having a holiday.

Go home and start to clean out kitchen cupboards.

Instruction from life-coach— *Remove all unnecessary clutter from life.*

Find almost-empty bottle of Christmas pudding brandy—shame to waste it…

Busybody Do-Gooding neighbour from three up knocks on open back door just as I am throwing now empty bottle into rubbish box. Am sitting on kitchen floor surrounded by 'to throw out' stuff. See from her expression that she has totally mis-judged the situation.

Try to tell her that I am simply following the advice of life-coach and discarding unnecessary clutter from my life—also upholding housewifely thrift of late mother-in-law—never throw away food or drink.

Try to assume control of situation and stand up to give self more authority. But brandy much stronger than I thought. Kitchen spins! Floor be-comes a Mount Everest-type incline impossible to stand straight on. Cling to sink whilst neighbour asks if I have ever thought of joining AA.

Am so offended that I deliberately pretend not to understand. Just because have thriftily drunk brandy does not make me an alcoholic!

Tell her that Derek has co-opted car, and so guaranteed home start provided by Automobile Association not really applicable. Talking of car reminds me that I had decided to get son's bike out of garage and use. V. trendy, and will look good on 'things to achieve' list. Can see self now, riding fearlessly into town. Will buy a crisp white shirt and some jeans and will look totally together and Oxbridge, my hair gleaming in the sunlight and my skin glowing with health.

Drift into beautiful brandy-induced daydream and can see myself looking sexily academic. Sexy new neighbour will see me and fall instantly and passionately in love!

Only one problem. Seem to remember son's bike one of those wheelie things. Suddenly also see hideous mental image of myself in blue cycling shorts to match poor cold blue legs and one of those ant-like helmets.

Do-Gooding neighbour is making tea. Says there's a good drop-in centre for people with problems like mine at the local church, and that the vicar is very modern.

On sudden unexpected impulse ask her if she has ever smoked a joint.

She looks puzzled, and then says she did do a smoked ham two years ago, for her Christmas Eve party, but that her husband thought it tasted too gamey. She could let me have the recipe, though. She keeps them all filed in a book, together with a note of when she made them. Apparently Delia told her to do that.

In daze hear myself earnestly explaining. No, I am talking about drugs. Things one should have done in life. Like having sex in public and taking drugs.

See she is beginning to look quite pale, so solicitously offer her a glass of the cooking sherry at back of cupboard. She tries to refuse, but I insist and pour her a glass. Assure her that sitting on floor is quite comfortable, and safer too, since floor is now at an acute angle.

Half an hour later have finished sherry, and the box of red wine left over from a dinner party. Neighbour is looking quite flushed.

Says she is sorry Derek has left.

Tell her I that am not sorry. That I am looking forward to being independent. (One of my life-coach statements that I am supposed to repeat every day.)

Neighbour confesses that her husband has not turned out to be the man she expected.

'He has his funny little ways, if you know what I mean,' she tells me. 'And I have tried to talk to him about them!'

Forcing my expression into one of good neighbourly sympathy and understanding, I listen, and ask if she'd like to talk about it.

To my shock, neighbour bursts into noisy tears and says she's sick of bloody talking about it. She wants to do it and it has come to that point where she has no option but to take matters into her own hands!

Even though I'm feeling a bit tipsy, I know immediately that this is not a subject I want to pursue.

So quickly and v. cleverly change it, and ask artlessly if anyone has moved into posh house at end of road as yet...

Neighbour's face immediately takes on worrying expression that reminds me of starving wild animal salivating at sight of fresh meat. Explains that A MAN has moved in ON HIS OWN—well, on his own apart from a v. undesirable and obviously out-for-what-she-can-get young female.

Neighbour explains that she's v. concerned for new man and feels that someone should warn and protect him. She has noticed from seeing washing hung up on line in back garden that he doesn't know how to hang out shirts properly, and that the plants on his patio need re-potting. She has decided to go round and offer her services.

Comment that I am surprised she has been able to see into back garden, since totally enclosed by ten-foot-high fence. Neighbour confides in whisper that actually she is able to see into garden from her bathroom window—if she stands in washbasin and cranes neck!

Confess to her that I find her sense of neighbourly concern and responsibility truly awesome.

Neighbour returns compliment by informing me that new man wears 'modern' you-know-whats.

Takes complicated and convoluted ten-minute conversation to discover she means underpants. I immediately start fantasising about new neighbour all over again—this time featuring in a Calvin Klein ad.

Neighbour is holding out her glass for more wine. Funny how I'd never realised before how much we have in common. Ask her if she has ever considered services of a life-coach.

Start to explain to her what one is, and stop when realise she isn't listening. Discover that the reason for her lack of response is that she is lying flat out on kitchen floor. Out of sisterly consideration I turn her on her side when she starts to snore.

Wake up from truly horrid dream in which I was sitting on kitchen floor drinking cleaning fluid with dreadful nosy parker neighbour from three doors up whilst sexy new neighbour went through whole strip routine from *Full Monty*! Thank God it was only a dream.

Phone rings. Pick it up.

Caller's my niece Georgie. Well, actually Derek's niece. Actually, she started life as Derek's nephew, but then in all honesty it never was clear right from the start just what he or she was. We all blamed the doctor who delivered George. Well, he wasn't really a doctor then, more of a medical student who was the conductor on the bus Derek's sister Alicia was travelling on. Afterwards, he—Travers—said that if he'd had a son with a widget as small as Georgie's he'd have been glad to have a doctor claim he was a girl to prevent him from suffering any embarrassment when the boy grew up.

Anyway, it all got sorted out in the end. Georgie had the operation ten years ago, and after that she really blossomed. It's amazing what hormones and a skilled hair-removal practitioner can do.

Georgie says she's heard the news about Derek and that she and her partner Erica want to come round and offer me their sisterly support.

It's Derek's own fault they've taken my side. Derek never did mange to hide his squeamishness when Georgie proudly showed him that jar with the widget in it.

Try to explain that I have pounding headache no doubt brought on by stress and grief. (Which life-coach has told me must be eradicated from my thought processes.)

I try also to remember what I am supposed to chant every morning, but then realise am going to be sick. Dash to the loo, and then realise that I have agreed to cook for Georgie and Erica this evening!

Three hours later am now feeling well enough to go to shops and buy something for Georgie and Erica to eat.

Remembering life-coach's stern warning that I must not let myself go, and that pride is equal to self-respect, I shower, put on best clothes and make-up.

This has nothing to do with fact that am going to walk past No. 14, of course. Am simply following life-coach's instructions!

Just get close to No. 14 when I suddenly feel sure I have seen beginnings of a run in tights. I put down basket and inspect my leg, casting surreptitious look towards drive of No. 14 at same time.

Obviously I would have made an excellent detective as I see immediately that expensive shiny black car is in the drive.

Unfortunately I do not see equally shiny and expensive young woman getting out of passenger side of it until hear her exclaim in anxious voice. 'Oh, Tate, look at that poor woman there. I think she must be feeling ill. Her face looks dreadfully red.'

Mortified, I stand up quickly—too quickly in view of delicate state of stomach. Red face must have been reflection from my skirt, 'cos it now feels very green.

Shiny expensive young woman is even more shiny and expensive at close quarters—bare, tanned legs, tight-fitting denim skirt clinging to the narrowest little hips I have even seen, bare, tanned midriff, thick glossy mane of streaked blonde hair…

Sexy man has protective hand under her elbow—no doubt afraid a breeze might blow her away. I see him frowning as he looks at me, so I make a grab for my basket and walk quickly away.

Suddenly feel very old and lonely—must be the red skirt. Personally, I never liked it. Derek chose it because it was in the sale…

At shops feel so low that am forced to buy huge block of chocolate with milk money, and decide Georgia and Erica will have to make do with spag bol from freezer.

Punish myself by walking long way home, so that I don't get to go past sexy man's house.

Get home and spend rest of afternoon getting ready for Georgie and Erica's visit.

Drink glass of red wine whilst cooking spag bol to cheer self up. Also take off red skirt and pull on comfy joggers and old shirt of Derek's with iron burn on back.

Heard the doorbell ring and go to answer it, yanking door back with wide smile and cheerful speech.

'Small willies must run in your family, because Derek's—'

Discover it's not Georgie and Erica standing outside, but new sexy neighbour!

Now my face *is* bright red! Neighbour glances back to where black shiny car is parked outside his house.

'I think you dropped this earlier,' he tells me in the most gorgeous sexy American accent I have ever heard, as he hands me dog-eared prescription for next lot of HRT! Must have fallen out of bag when I checked tights.

Out of corner of my eye, see Georgie's car pull up. It's an ancient Beetle covered in many battle wounds, which she drives with total disregard for law and traffic.

Georgie gets out accompanied by Erica. Erica is inflated by v. obvious baby bulge.

I am too shocked to be able to reply coherently to neighbour, who is now walking back to his own house, whilst Georgie carefully shepherds Erica up the path.

'We've got a surprise for you.' Georgie beams as soon as they get into the house. 'Erica is pregnant.'

Am not sure what to say, so offer weak smile.

Once in kitchen Georgie and Erica explain that the baby's father has been chosen carefully so that baby will grow up with no sexual hang-ups. Georgie informs me that sperm donor chosen by them has incredibly high IQ, so baby will probably win Nobel prize and become an icon others will turn to for inspiration.

Erica gives me a dreamy look and adds that donor also six foot three, blond-haired, and a superb athlete.

Start to feel slightly anxious about the distinct *froideur* in the air as parents-to-be begin a polite and earnest discussion about the relative merits of brain over brawn. Erica gets my vote when she says there's no reason why their son shouldn't have both.

Further earnest discussion ensues about the colour scheme for the nursery. I put television on to catch up with soaps and give them privacy to discuss in peace, but Georgie requests that it be turned off. Apparently they are afraid of baby being contaminated by rubbishy TV programmes and are only allowing him to hear sounds that educate and enlighten him.

Must be red wine that entices me to comment that he must have found argument between them about colour of nursery very enlightening.

When Georgie sulks she looks very like Derek. Feel glad for baby's sake that it was fathered by donated sperm.

However, immediately feel v. guilty when, after spag bol—Erica is only eating organic food from known recommended sources—Georgie announces that they want me to be an older adult member of the baby's specially-chosen life circle of non-biological family.

Georgie and Erica ask about my plans for future. I explain about lack of money and necessity of having to get a job. Also tell them that Derek is determined to sell house.

Georgie immediately denounces Derek and says I must not give in to him. Point out that I don't have much choice—house has huge mortgage and I have no money.

Georgie suggests I could bring in some income by letting out the spare bedrooms. Seems that with upgrading and expansion of local university to include new 'Change Career Mid-life' courses there is huge demand for temporary accommodation from mature students. Georgie works for local university in administration and KNOWS ABOUT THESE THINGS!

She offers to vet prospective lodgers and send some round! She also gives me kind hint that modern mature students have more sophisticated tastes than in my day, and spag bol is not an ideal dish to put on menu!

Erica kindly suggests I should upgrade image, saying Nigella Lawson image very popular with more mature man!

Point out that I am considerably older than Domestic Goddess, and hair is considerably shorter.

Erica agrees, but asks if I have thought of investing in good bra! Apparently she has recently seen TV programme showing that most women do not know their own bra size.

Take a deep breath and manage—just—not to point out that own problem has nothing to do with bra size but effect of time, gravity and two breast-fed babies!

After Georgie and Erica have gone I drink a large glass of wine and eat a bowl of spag bol. Then realise that if am to take in lodgers will have to sort out spare bedrooms!

CHAPTER FOUR

TODAY I am having a garage sale of all my accumulated baggage. Once gone, my life will be streamlined and uncluttered. Along with material baggage I will have got rid of all unwanted emotional baggage. (Life-coach lesson No. 4.) I can then start to get bedrooms ready for potential lodgers.

Have heard from old Mr Russell two doors down that nosy parker Do-Gooding neighbour has gone down with strange virus.

It can't be any stranger than weird dreams I keep on having about her. Last night she was standing in her back garden stark naked, cooking a piece of meat over an open fire.

Am deriving much satisfaction from selling all Derek's possessions, including his bottle-top collection and scratched records. Just wish it would stop raining, though. Garage is too full of stuff for people to come in out of rain.

Hope to make enough to pay huge telephone bill that I found stuffed at back of bill drawer.

Building society have been on phone to say that husband has handed them a signed letter to say that I am now sole owner of house—along with them.

After allowing time for me to stop whimpering with shock, building society person assured me kindly that after house sale there should not be too much of a shortfall and that they will give me time to make repayments. How kind!

Son rang this morning to say he is going on a historical dig and that he is sending me something to remind me of his father!

Son also wanted to know what father's new address would be so that he could visit him in summer hols. Oh, and apparently his student loan is now £12,000 and his bank is demanding that he repays his £1,000 overdraft. Can I let him have a cheque?

Daughter also rang very miffed. Apparently she has been having trouble getting her live-in partner, Brian, to commit. She had told him how good our marriage was, et cetera, et cetera, and had just about talked him round into agreeing to visit us.

Brian doesn't believe in families, which is why for the five years they have lived together they have never once visited us.

She feels that her father and I could at least have waited until after she and Brian had gone through the very special bonding ceremony she had just about persuaded him in to.

Apparently it was to have taken place on a very remote island—to signify Brian's total rejection of everything material. (He's an artist, so doesn't work, and she supports them both—which she doesn't mind because she wants to be the muse behind his genius.) There was a problem, though, because Brian wanted to write a piece of special music to celebrate the mystical union of oneness that is life in its purest form (always thought life in its purest form was the amoeba, but perhaps I'm wrong). Daughter wasn't sure they could hire the equipment to drive the waves onto the beach with the right rhythmic frequency.

Offer to send her a copy of my '30 things to do' list—underlining the relationship break-up number!

Have just left garage sale in capable hands of old Mr Russell to come inside for a necessary 'call of nature' and a bar of chocolate.

When I return Mr Russell advises me to call police since v. suspicious-looking man is skulking around garage. Apparently he's wearing an old mac and a balaclava. Panic that it might not be quite legal to be selling son's old airgun. Have seen warnings on *Police File* about dangerous crims always on look-out for firearms.

Mr Russell offers to go home for his dog. Politely refuse. Dog, Sheba, is known to have a predilection for human male flesh—especially off the buttocks. Have enough financial problems already without being sued!

Building society ring again. They are being very kind. I can stay in house for another three months! Also, equally kindly, they point out an extra loan I hadn't realised husband had taken out. However, there is good news. They have found an old joint account we had forgotten we opened—apparently it has just over £100 in it.

Have just seen Mr Russell's suspicious-looking character. I watch as he shuffles to back of garage and then follow him discreetly.

Shock horror—he's trying to steal Derek's bottle-tops. I am just about to call for help when I see he's also wearing Derek's signet ring. Double check and realise it is Derek!

Two hours later Derek is still pacing living room, wringing hands in anguish, unable to believe I could have tried to sell his treasures. We have long heated discussion about the differences between valuable artefacts worth treasuring and rubbish. Just like old times.

Point out to Derek that I have no money, and—since he has just told me that would-be buyer has withdrawn from sale negotiations—house is still not sold.

Eventually agree to let Derek have 'treasures' in return for the fifty-three pounds and eight pence he has in his pocket. That, with money received from garage sale, means I now have sum of £75.20p.

On his way out Derek stops to give me a reluctant kiss on cheek. Not sure whether to laugh or cry. Don't particularly want a passionate snog with him, if honest, but still hurts to see relief in his eyes as he steps back. I might not have over-inflated breasts and an under-inflated IQ, but we had our moments—all right, then, seconds.

Oh, also forget to tell Derek that we have been invited to a Silver Wedding party at a house around the corner.

After Derek has gone I go out to garage to clear up remnants of sale. Everything is wet, dirty and miserable. Pick up broken glass from garage floor and realise it is black cat Derek and I bought on honeymoon for good luck.

Just finishing sweeping up bits when I see sexy new neighbour driving past. Equally sexy blonde girl is sitting in passenger seat of car.

Realise reason for suddenly blurred vision not some life-threatening sinister manifestation of my increasing age, but is because I am crying!

CHAPTER FIVE

RECEIVED e-mail from mother. She says she is coming over to visit me and that something needs to be sacrificed. Start to panic. Thought she'd given that sort of thing up when she divorced husband number three.

Today am having lunch with Jacki and Rosie and other abandoned wives, at local pub.

Rosie is one of the organisers of new group set up in town to help discarded middle-aged women like me regain confidence and social skills. Aim is to meet up once a month for confidence-boosting, emotion-sharing and in-depth discussions. Sounds very high-minded and serious and I am not sure I will fit in.

Jacki rings at nine-thirty to say that she has persuaded Rosie to have meeting at trendy new wine bar just opened in originally stuffy but now modernised country club.

Privately feel dubious as country club is also home of local impossible-to-get-into county set golf club which has strict 'no women in bar' policy.

However, Jacki insists. Claims new bar is full of mature 'suits' and I should be sure to wear something sexy.

I remember that only sexy item in my wardrobe was the scratchy black lace crotchless number Derek bought for me one Christmas on train coming home from work after Christmas party, from another man who was having second thoughts about its suitability for his wife.

Anyway, it was stolen from the washing line when Derek's mother found it and put it in a whites wash by mistake, thus ruining all Derek's work shirts.

Also not sure trendy wine bar is sort of place discarded old women should be going to try to bond and regain confidence.

Spend all morning trying on everything in wardrobe and then discarding each item—twice. In the end I have narrowed choice down to two items—best red skirt or sensible chainstore black trouser suit which I got in sale 'cos one leg is shorter than other (on trousers, not me).

Opt for trouser suit and white tee shirt—well, was white once—is now sort of yellow-greyish-white, but at least can wear back to front so that faded red wine stain won't show.

One slight problem. Have now lost weight, due to trauma of being replaced by Cheree. Trousers so loose that I have to put string through belt loops to pull them in.

Arrive at wine bar to find Jacki and Rosie already there. Both notice I have lost weight, and Rosie asks if it's true that when one is old and losing weight one ends up with dangling folds of loose skin. Jacki says she knows of a wonderful surgeon for that sort of thing. I huffily deny any need for same. Any slight lack of skintone can soon be put right by normal exercise.

(Resolve to buy v. wide elastic bandage.)

Jacki wearing brand-new pristine designer white trouser suit with nothing under jacket—just like film star.

Rosie is wearing 'antique' beaded top found in street market and new trousers. Feel mortified to realise I am scruffiest and worst-dressed person there!

Quick glance at menu and heart starts to pound in shock.

Feel sure must have been a printing mistake and an extra zero has been added to all prices!

Jacki orders a bottle of wine.

Quickly empty own glass and say airily that I am not having anything to eat as am having a fasting day.

Jacki says wine is her treat, so I drink another glass in relief.

See one of 'suits' leering down Jacki's cleavage. He looks about fifteen and sounds as if voice hasn't broken properly!

Rosie drags me over to meet other sad, discarded people. I follow her through crowd, trying to wriggle past noisy group of loud women in killer heels, short skirts and low-cut tops, heckling poor young male waiter for not being quick enough with drinks.

Shocked to discover this is group of sad discards! Vaguely recognise one of them, who turns out to be divorced wife of snotty golf club president.

I remember seeing her photograph in the paper, driving expensive Rolls Royce car over golf course and pinning now ex-husband to a tree.

However, when I whisper this to Rosie I am told that situation was totally misreported by local male-dominated press and that ex-wife was not drunk and abusive, as claimed, but was generously supporting the cause of women by underlining the essential selfishness of a male-dominated sport that forces men to choose between it and the loving company of adoring wives. It was not her fault that her ex-husband was shamefully taken over by the need to hit little balls with piece of metal, and so didn't realise pain that he'd caused his devoted helpmate and partner!

Rosie is indignant that woman's now ex-husband is the one who needs counselling for his addiction, not loyal wife who simply wanted him to come home for his dinner. Since she was precluded from entering the bar she had no choice but to draw his attention to the overcooked meal by driving onto golf course. Just another example of the way facts are twisted in favour of powerful lobbyists instead of being reported truthfully.

Feel perhaps it's not a good idea to mention that the newspaper also mentioned the ex-wife developed Uri Geller-type skill in bending husband's golf clubs before throwing them and him into expensive water feature. Unfortunately the swans were mating, and a male swan got jealous and attacked the husband.

I am introduced to the group and accept a welcome drink. I wonder when we will be going somewhere quiet to bond and have in-depth discussion referred to by Rosie, but am too polite to ask.

I am fascinated by smooth, unlined face of golf club president's ex-wife and fearsome way she doesn't frown—at all.

Rosie explains discreetly that she has had Botox treatment at Botox party. Jacki comes up and overhears. Informs me that she is planning to have own Botox party, and makes generous offer that I should be party guinea pig and get the treatment free.

'Of course, everyone will have to have a go at injecting your lines, just to see what happens, but that's okay because you've got plenty. And you needn't worry if they don't get the needle in quite right—the effect only lasts three months.'

I smile wanly and accept another drink. My head is feeling distinctly muzzy and I can hear loud cheering before I am caught up in sudden surge of killer-heeled women herding towards exit.

I assume we are now going to bond and have in-depth discussions, until Rosie explains that golf club president's ex has just raised a motion that we assert ourselves and breach the illegal dominance of male culture which is rife in the area, and that all the other women are in favour.

Still completely puzzled.

Jacki explains that they are going to break in to exclusive all-male golf club bar!!

As the hordes rush past I am overwhelmed by fumes of alcohol and perfume, plus the heady nectar of female power throwing off male oppression.

It's a pity about the little male waiter getting trampled on, and I have to be honest I don't think it was really necessary for that huge tennis-playing champion to rip off his shirt and tell him to let everything hang out. But I'm sure his mother will understand why he ended up with underpants on his head, and be proud of the role he played in the revolution.

Golf club bar is mysteriously empty—but the game is given away by swinging of door leading to hallowed all-male territory of the snooker room.

Tennis player leads the stampede, magnificently supported by golf club president's ex and local Guide leader.

V. heady moment when doors finally give way and prey is spotted quivering behind snooker table.

Must say I am impressed by the snooker skills of golf club president's ex—her aim is unerring as she manages to pot balls in correct order. The sight of golf club dignitaries cowering behind the table with coloured balls in their mouths and hands over their family jewels will make a very good photograph.

What a triumph! I feel quite euphoric about it all…can even hear bells ringing…

Feel brutal tug on arm by Jacki.

'Come on,' she demands. 'Can't you hear the police sirens?'

There is a mad rush for the exit which is blocked by bar steward.

A shiver runs down my spine as I see the way golf club president's wife paws the floor. Also hear knuckles of tennis player cracking.

'Ladies, please…' bar steward implores.

That does it. President's ex is almost foaming at mouth.

'We are not ladies,' she roars. 'Now, get out of our way, otherwise—'

I am not sure what would have happened if police hadn't arrived!

Have to say police were v. understanding.

I find out later that Chief Constable is in contention with golf club president about the outcome of v. important golf match, which president claims to have won. Also an unsubstantiated rumour that golf president's ex nobly sacrificed herself for the sake of rest of us and offered police chief sex in return for our release. I am sure this is not true.

It was a bit embarrassing when Jacki suddenly announced, 'Right girls!' pulled off her jacket to reveal her chest—and then threw jacket at police officer now guarding exit.

I am sure she didn't mean to run straight into his arms, and she couldn't have known that a photographer would be there and a photograph of her topless with the policeman would appear in local paper.

As we were all ushered towards waiting police vans I saw a familiar face amongst the group of golfers walking towards club house.

Realised it was sexy new neighbour, and immediately prayed he would not recognise me.

Tell myself I am behaving like silly schoolgirl—but can't help it…

New neighbour is quite definitely sexiest man on earth!

Later see nosy neighbour from three up peering out from behind her curtains when I am helped from taxi by solicitous old lady who saw me trying to cross busy main road after too many drinks. (Of course I'd had to celebrate being let off by police with newly discovered soulmates.)

CHAPTER SIX

WAKE up with thick head to hear loud knocking at front door. Have taken to wearing Derek's pyjamas in bed—not 'cos they remind me of him, but because they are warm.

The bottoms fall down as I hurry downstairs to answer imperative summons on door, so discard them. Hug the pyjama jacket round my body as I unlock door and peer round. I discover sinisterly grinning new postman standing on step, holding a parcel.

Put hand round door to retrieve, but postman snatches it back. Parcel apparently has to be signed for. If don't will have to call at post office to collect.

I edge cautiously round door, conscious of neighbours and the fact that my only item of apparel is a pyjama jacket with no buttons. Postman is really smirking now. I think at first it must be because he's after my body, but then realise that's highly unlikely, and see that anyway postman is looking at semi-open parcel.

Anxious to get rid of him, so quickly scrawl signature and grab parcel and letters. Unfortunately grab wrong end of parcel, and contents start to emerge.

At first can't work out just what fluorescent rubber thing is, and assume must be some kind of free soap powder gift. But then see that it is actually obscenely disgusting vibrator of proportions unfit to be discussed.

Feeling faint with shock and totally mortified, I slam door.

I realise that this must be promised gift from son—if so son has more of his father in him than had known. Obviously he has inherited his father's sense of humour! But am even more concerned by son's appalling lack of taste and colour sensitivity.

I take vibrator into kitchen and discard packaging in the bin. Am halfway back upstairs when telephone rings. Caller is stepsister, ringing to say that a friend of hers, a reporter working for popular national newspaper, has been commissioned to write an article on the work of my wonderfully successful life-coach!

According to my stepsister, life-coach has volunteered me for article as a typical under-achieving client on whom she has wrought a miracle transformation—turned sow's ear into beautiful silk purse etc. To prove how good she is, newspaper is prepared to pay for a total makeover for me, including new clothes for photographs to accompany the article. Paper will pay for everything. All I have to do is be interviewed.

Life-coach has sent bossy message via stepsister saying I must have put together a list of the things I want to achieve! My stepsister demands that I send it to life-coach immediately, and she will let me know when life-coach wants to see me and discuss what I will say to reporter when interviewed.

I fail to mention my list is most unsuitable for public viewing!

I get showered and dressed and I am halfway through breakfast when phone rings again. This time it's Georgie saying that she has given my address and telephone number to a potential lodger who will be ringing to make an appointment. I daren't ask too many questions in case they appear non-politically correct. All I know is potential tenant is aged thirty-four and male. Oh, also seems prepared to pay potentially enormous amount of money for room!

Quickly multiply sum by four, since house has five bedrooms, and realise this will easily cover mortgage payments! Suddenly realise the temptation to fill single rooms with ten beds, but remind myself that it is totally wrong to profit from human suffering. Wonder if I should say same to building society?

*   *   *

Later—totally unexpectedly I am now temporary owner of old Mr Russell's dog. Mr Russel was rushed into hospital with suspected food poisoning from eating an out-of-date can of dog food by mistake; had been given to him by local charity. The dog, apparently, can open fridge, and had pinched chicken intended for Mr Russell's dinner. Social Services say dog has to be put down if kind-hearted neighbour with nothing better to do doesn't take it in.

Social Services dragon points out that walking is very healthy for a woman of my age.

Dog, which goes by the name of Sheba (as in queen of), and I confront one another over no woman's territory of kitchen. Dog has staked out claim on areas in front of fridge and Aga. On mat in front of Aga is a pack of fat-free yoghurts, un-eaten but punched with teeth-marks, fridge door is open—I see she has rejected a piece of hard old cheese. Since I now have no yoghurts I will have to have cheese for my own supper!

I tell her if she doesn't mend her ways I will cut off all her pretty hair and then she will look old and frumpy—just like me.

Later still—would-be tenant has just arrived. Unexpectedly he looks normal and clean. He's a mature student at university who, having made a fortune doing something clever with computers, can now afford to indulge himself by getting an education. I show him his room, and am just explaining house rules, like no overnight visitors without prior agreement etc., when dog sidles in, jumps on bed and proceeds to pick fleas off her fur.

I am mortified, but at least now know cause of the strange rash round my ankles. I had thought it was another manifestation of natural grief and stress over discovery of husband's infidelity.

Husband rings. Sounds as though he is speaking through a wad of damp tissues—perhaps he is. Wants to know if anyone has been round looking for him. Tell him no, and ask if this a good time to talk about son's overdraft and daughter's relationship problems, not to mention my mother's impending visit, but he hangs up.

Would-be lodger rings to confirm he wants room.

Son's bank rings to confirm that I am going to repay his overdraft.

Go to bed early, worn out by excitement of day—plus head still pounding from previous day's overexcitement.

Am having a wonderful dream: sliding fingers through lovely silky chest hair of sexy elder brother of Russell Crowe. Mmm… He is now nuzzling my ear. Love the sound of that heavy breathing. Mmm…

Suddenly wake up to discover dog is lying on bed next to me. Am mortified when dog gives me a mistrustful look and gets up. It wasn't my fault. She shouldn't be upstairs anyway.

Dog is obviously missing Mr Russell and has lost her appetite. She totally refuses tinned food and I am having to tempt her with little treats.

Must say am finding it very comforting to have someone appreciative to cook for again—no, not lodger; he has not moved in yet. Makes me very sad person, but am now cooking delicious dinners for dog. Have found out she does not eat doggy junk food but prefers wholesome home cooking, preferably involving large quantities of meat.

Am now on hugely fashionable Atkins diet, eating enormous portions of protein.

I remember that I haven't sent the list of intended achievements to life-coach. Eventually find it amongst papers on kitchen table.

Manage to finish cleaning lodger's room. New credit card arrives in post for Derek—have forged his signature and used it to stock up with food for lodger and buy new towels etc.

Also posted list to life-coach!

I am to take dog for a walk this afternoon. Have decided we both need exercise. Life-coach notes say that healthy exercise produces positive, forward-looking mind.

I am feeling a wonderfully proud temporary dog owner. Dog walks beautifully at my side, carrying her own lead on my command. I look down my nose at other less fortunate dog-walkers, whose pets are obviously not under control.

Have had to wear daughter's discarded jeans since my own clothes are falling off…had to struggle a little with zip, but breathing in will tighten flabby stomach.

A couple walking a strange-looking thing a bit like a floor mop on wheels pause to look apprehensively at Sheba. I coo reassuringly that she is perfectly behaved, but to my horror Sheba leaps on top of floor mop and tries to mate with it!

Woman screams and so does Floor Mop. I firmly call Sheba off. Couple try to pull Floor Mop away, but Sheba bares her teeth at them.

I tell the man reassuringly that all is well since she has had the operation…

Floor Mop and woman are both now hysterical, and a crowd is now starting to gather. All are offering advice, including sending for a man with a gun to shoot Sheba.

I am totally and absolutely mortified.

Out of corner of my eye see a man standing watching. He has an immaculate chocolate

Labrador on lead. OHMYGOD! Shock, horror—it is sexy new neighbour!! Watch as he walks up to Sheba and holds out his closed hand. Miraculously she gets off Floor Mop and follows him. He brings her to my side and opens hands.

'I find these work wonders,' he tells me kindly in deep, deep rich velvet very masculine voice that makes arms all goosebumpy and he hands me some doggie treats.

Sheba is now eying his dog appreciatively.

I lunge out to grab her and realise zip has burst on my jeans, revealing flabby stomach encased in horrid old knickers. I think I am about to faint with reaction.

Sexy new neighbour suggests a cup of restorative coffee!!

I try to explain that Sheba is not actually my dog, that I am simply doing someone a favour. Then hear another woman saying Sheba and owner are both as bad as each other. I feel even more mortified.

Refuse kind offer of coffee and go home.

Am in love, totally and absolutely. In fact feel like a girl again—only more so!! (Much more so!!)

Doorbell rings and heart flips over. Not sexy neighbour, though, but new lodger.

Sheba greets him like old friend. Take tenant upstairs and ask politely if will be needing an evening meal.

Tenant says he has a better idea. Why don't we go out to eat? Suspect Georgie warned him about the spag bol.

Accept very kind invitation.

Have dinner in expensive local eatery and exchange brief life histories with tenant.

Learn he was in long-term relationship that broke down when girlfriend went to work in New York. (So he's hetero, then! Though he's really not my type—perhaps my daughter would be interested?) He explains that his parents have retired to live in Italy and that his sister and family live in Australia. While he's doing this course he's happy to rent a room before he decides where he wants to settle.

I tell him about my own family background, but not in too much detail. Don't want him to move straight out again!

I explain about up-coming interview with life-coach and necessity of finding a job if am to keep house and pay off debts. I am thinking of applying for telephone call centre job—soothing angry customers.

We are just getting up to leave when I see that sexy new neighbour is also in restaurant. Alone.

SNN sees me and comes over. I introduce him to tenant. SNN makes pleasant social chit-chat and enquires after Sheba. He explains that Labrador belongs to a friend and that he works for a large American corporation which has offices locally.

He mentions that he has been invited to neighbour's silver wedding bash, and that he is looking forward to meeting everyone—especially the astronomer at No. 6. When I look blank, he explains that he has seen her looking through a telescope.

Realise he is talking about the nosy neighbour from three up! I just manage to refrain from saying that the only stars she is interested in are those on the pages of *Hello!* (Hadn't realised nosy neighbour had telescope. That must be how she was able to read logo on SNN's close-fit underwear!)

Firmly tell myself not to allow thoughts to travel down that road. Can actually feel face and body becoming overheated!

Go to ladies' to powder nose, leaving two men to talk cars.

Walk back slowly, head in air, ignoring the looks I am getting from other diners. Can't wait for promised new outfit, especially now I am two sizes smaller. My grandmother was right after all about clouds having silver linings!

As I reach our table SNN is just leaving. He takes a few steps and then comes back, looking deep into my eyes whilst my heart pounds. SNN lowers head and begins to whisper in my ear! Am in heaven!!

Then realise he is delicately telling me that skirt is caught up in knickers!! Even worse follows when he laughs and says that I remind him of his grandmother!!!

Get home to discover that forgot to padlock fridge and dog has raided again. New lodger v. understanding and says that he's sure that once bacon she has left has been washed it will be perfectly okay for breakfast!

Must say I am really enjoying company of tenant, who is upgrading my computer skills.

I arrived home from visiting old Mr Russell in hospital to report on health and mental wellbeing of dog, to find postman had left a parcel. Opened it and discovered inside a huge pile of son's dirty washing, and a note saying, 'Told you this would remind you of Dad!'

I am just holding pile at arm's length and putting it in machine when see nosy neighbour from three up approaching back door in v. furtive manner.

I open door and let her in.

She immediately asks in urgent whisper if a parcel has been delivered to me for her; only she has given my address as she doesn't want her husband to know that she has sent for an item for personal growth as husband is old-fashioned about such things.

At first I am confused, and ask if this item has something to do with her new interest in astronomy, as SNN had mentioned to me.

Neighbour's face goes v. unflattering shade of puce and she immediately denies any interest in rubbishy things like horoscopes—although she does feel that my husband and I are not exactly soulmates as natal charts are in conflict.

Explain that I am referring to science of astronomy, not astrology, and ask if she has seen any interesting formations in the night sky through her telescope set up in bathroom.

Neighbour now having trouble breathing. She says shortly that telescope belongs to husband, and demands to know if parcel has been delivered for her or not, as is vital that she knows where undelivered personal growth item might have gone.

Suddenly have a flash of insight and realise that nosy neighbour is talking about grotesque fluorescent green vibrator!!!

Haughtily announce that said parcel was delivered by inanely grinning postman, and had been opened in transit. Further announce that mine is a decent respectable house and item in question was immediately consigned to rubbish bin.

Nosy neighbour flies into temper and accuses me of misappropriating contents of parcel for my own use!

Traumatised by whole episode, I tell neighbour theatrically never to darken my door again unless she apologises. Say sweetly as I open the door and wait for her to leave that I will search through rubbish and deliver vibrator personally to her door—add that I am sure her husband will be thrilled by its safe arrival! Smile as neighbour totters off!

CHAPTER SEVEN

TODAY I am to travel to London to have interview with life-coach and newspaper reporter.

Have to wear black trouser suit as I have nothing else in wardrobe, and spend pleasant two hours on train daydreaming about showing off wonderfully slimmed-down figure in stunning designer outfit that makes me look like top model. (Train journey actually only takes thirty-five minutes, but there is a problem on the line—problem is obviously too dreadfully worrying for the sensitive ears of nervous passengers, as no announcement is made to explain why we have not moved for over an hour!)

Eventually reach destination very late for appointment!

Life-coach is not amused. Well, assume she is not—hard to tell since her face is devoid of any kind of expression. I'm desperate to ask if she has attended one of Jacki's Botox parties, but am too afraid. Life-coach reminds me of stern games teacher at school, who refused to force me into loathsome cross-country runs.

Stepsister informs me in anguished whisper that life-coach is still in shock after receipt of my goals list.

Life-coach finally deigns to speak to me and announces coldly that she presumes my list was a childish joke and so she has substituted a more suitable list of her own to the reporter.

She presents me with a copy of the substitute list—I start to object that it is boring and pretentious, but am being hustled away by stepsister and PR person for makeover.

Two hours later am totally 'made-over', and feel like an actress in a part I haven't learned any lines for.

PR person has had 'cool' idea of making my new image fit pretentious and boring list supplied by life-coach.

Now look like cross between 1930s ageing virginal spinster and sinister psychotic character from chilling thriller film.

Oh, and the Meg Ryan look-alike hairstyle I had requested for makeover is a total disaster and reminds me bitterly of previous equally disastrous attempts to reinvent my life by way of a change of hairdo!!

As I am reduced to tears by horrid sight in the mirror, I see first signs of emotion in life-coach's face as triumphant smile stretches mouth.

Oh, almost forgot—I get to keep special new outfit chosen for photoshoot!

Later, when I have been removed from hallowed presence of life-coach and allowed to give vent to feelings, stepsister flies into temper and calls me an ungrateful cow.

Which is all very well, but ask how she would like to wear thick woolly knee-high socks, a short pleated skirt in yellow and purple check tartan with an elasticated waist, and a sleeveless polo neck top three sizes too small which reveals truly hideous sight of aging upper arm flesh.

Stepsister too shocked by my ingratitude to speak at first, but then reveals that outfit was donated specially for the occasion by an up-and-coming new designer.

I say am going to change into my own too-big trouser suit in ladies' and go home. Stepsister says not possible as suit has been thrown in office shredding machine!

We part with mutual lack of empathy!

On way home I pop into chainstore, braving looks of other shoppers and staff, and buy new jeans and two tee shirts plus jacket. I pay with Derek's credit card, which I just happen to have in my purse, but afterwards feel so guilty that I make a vow to repay money from lodger's rent cheque.

Just make it back in time to get to interview for call centre job!

Good news!!!

I have got a job performing vitally important social function. Am to be 'valued member of

highly trained self-motivated team, earning potentially huge amounts of money'.

I will be working on a telephone sex line—and
I start training tomorrow!

I protest to grandmotherly supervisor that I'm
not really qualified for this sort of work.

'You've been married haven't you?' she asks.
'So you must know how to fake an orgasm!'

'Oooohhhhhhhh—yes, *yes*— YES…' I reply.

Get home to find friend Rosie has telephoned.
To make up for unpleasant incident at golf club
she has paid for us to join new trendy Schooldays-
r-Us internet thingy so that we can while away
lonely nights sending chatty e-mails to fellow for-
mer pupils.

She says it's best initially to identify oneself to
fellow pupils by classroom nickname, and generously reminds me that Jacki was known as
'Martini' and I as 'Don't Go There'.

Thoroughly miffed, I point out that actually I
was known as DGT, which stood for 'Damn Good
Time'. But she is laughing too much to listen.

Phone rings again. This time it's daughter.
Thanks to me, everything is all over with Brian
and she has now decided to come home and to re-
evaluate her life!

I remind daughter anxiously that she would be
foolish to give up a good job, but apparently I am
too late with motherly advice as she was forced to

give notice when new young male clerk misunderstood daughter's body language and accused her of sexual harassment!

Sympathise, but have to end call 'cos lodger, Daniel, has just popped head round kitchen door to say he has made himself and dog a beef stir fry and I am welcome to share if I want to.

What an absolute sweetie Daniel is!! Not that I am attracted to him personally—he's far too young and boyish for one thing—much prefer men of own age, just like sexy new neighbour, but would love to adopt Daniel as an extra son—or, better still, as son-in-law!!

Daniel wonderful—not only made supper but cleaned up afterwards as well. He has confessed that he has always enjoyed cooking but previous long-term partner was a model and didn't eat much. He confessed that he's beginning to suffer from pangs of paternal longing!! All he wants is to be a dad!

Am more and more convinced that Daniel is the perfect man for my own daughter!!

I tell him about my new career opportunity, and my fears that I am not suitably qualified.

Daniel blushes a little, then helpfully suggests that I watch 'adult' channels on cable TV for inspiration and shows me how to tune in.

Once over initial confusion about what exactly is going on, 'cos of close-up camera work and un-identifiable body parts, quite enjoy risqué sensation of watching naughty sex antics whilst drinking cocoa. Haven't laughed so much in ages—sad how watching normal non-actor-type human beings having sex is so mirth-provoking. Dog is a nuisance, though, as she sits in front of screen and howls.

Over cocoa confess to Daniel that I am worried about daughter's imminent return—although pleased about her break-up with Brian. Add semi-carelessly that daughter is longing to settle down and become a mother. (Not sure about the mother bit, but I am certainly looking forward to grand-children!!) After all, there's no harm in dropping careful discreet hints, and, just to make sure I am making the point clear enough, I add that I already feel as close to Daniel as if he were my own son!

Daniel confides that his own mother is a free spirit, now living somewhere in outer Knightsbridge with her latest lover, and that Daniel had to parent her more than she did him.

Have just staggered away from 'training' session for new job.

Training session involved sitting in with experienced sex line operator who is dominatrix!

Am sure third caller was golf club president—he wanted to be told to dress up in apron and nothing else and be forced to clean bathroom. He had to be told that tiles were not shiny enough and would have bare backside beaten with toilet brush.

I got told off by manager, who didn't like my unprofessional reaction to demands of callers. Apparently I could get fired for laughing so hard!! Also discovered that operators who earn the most are those with regular callers who specialise in specific type of sex.

Feel work is not exactly compatible with my views on life, but morning post brought mega-sized unpaid bills.

Manager kindly suggested that I might consider starting off with something not too challenging—apparently lots of callers like the thought of a raunchy woman opening door to them dressed in stockings. Manager suggested improvisation along these lines and I was generously offered opportunity to take next call!!

Opted to work from home, and agreed that equipment (phone, etc.) will be installed asap. Sent home to work on 'characters and storylines'.

At home switch on computer and discover have e-mail. Rosie has kindly left notes on Schooldays-r-Us site purporting to be from me, and using abbreviated nickname.

E-mail full of tender reminiscences about me and sender's youthful adoration—also refers to fact that he knew of my secret pash for him. Caller has signed off with nickname 'BB'.

Am immediately transported back to schooldays and raw passion of hormone-crazed lust for 'Big Boy', the captain of the football team. How touching that he felt the same for me!! Especially since he always used to make fun of me when at school.

Quickly go into site and discover that a reunion is being planned. Enthusiastically put down my nickname, and wonder if can possibly get a decent wig to hide hideous sour yellow and brown hairstyle which looks like dying chrysanthemum.

Have also received e-mail from daughter announcing that she's returning home at weekend.

Tonight Daniel is cooking marinated chicken brochettes with green couscous, followed by low-fat squidgy chocolate cakes.

Delicious!

The paper comes out today, with article about me in it. Have to search though it five times before realise photo of squinty seventy-year-old in bad wig is me!

Realise now what beauty contestants must go through when I read about my ambitions and life goals. Am amazed to read the generous praise which I have apparently heaped on the wonderful life-changing services of the life-coach after her total transformation of me.

Phone rings. It's a person asking for husband. This is the fifth call this week! Explain husband no longer lives here and give his new address. I neglect to mention that I haven't been able to reach Derek on his mobile or at his address for over a week.

Post arrives. Open it all and realise too late one envelope was addressed only to Derek.

Contains v. large cheque from an insurance policy I never knew he had.

Two hours later—of course I will tell Derek when I am able to make contact with him that cheque has arrived and is now safely in our old joint account at building society. Just as a precaution, I instruct society to close account once cheque has been cleared and use money to reduce mortgage. Manager is understanding and amenable.

One day later—have found out Derek has left country—because a man came round asking for money he says Derek owes him!

Can't believe it. SNN man has called round. Apparently he saw article in paper and recognised me! He said he found article most interesting.

Have to invite him in, of course.

Over coffee Tate tells me that he's divorced, with no children, and that the stunning blonde is his goddaughter!!!!!

I confide to him that the list in paper is not really my own and I never have had any ambitions to read Proust. Explain about life-coach and show Tate list torn from mag.

Dog has been beside Aga chewing something, but now comes over to Tate.

Dog has dropped grotesque fluorescent chewed vibrator at Tate's feet—unfortunately isn't chewed enough not to be recognisable as a vibrator. Am totally mortified and want to die.

Explain immediately that it's not mine and is in fact rightful property of nosy neighbour with husband with funny little ways.

Tate is wonderfully soothing, but I can see his shoulders heaving. He's obviously totally nauseated by whole thing.

To utter consternation I suddenly burst into tears and start to sob that life is unfair. Why do men always want women with big false boobs when own boobs look so awful?

Hear Tate reassuring me that my boobs look very nice.

'No.' Sob even more loudly. 'Are truly awful— look—'

Suddenly realise I am standing in own kitchen with shirt unfastened flashing boobs to sexy new neighbour!!! No wonder he has gone quiet and is clenching his jaw!!!

Start to gabble apology as Tate's mobile rings. He answers call and explains that caller is god-daughter, who wants him to pick her up from nail manicure bar as she doesn't want to risk her own nails by driving herself.

See Tate to door and then on way back catch sight of own reflection in mirror.

Mascara has run and I look like raddled old clown!!! In fact I look worse!!

See that light is flashing on newly installed sex line phone. Pick up receiver in really vile bad temper and tell heavy breather on other end that he should be locked up and key thrown away. Shockingly, caller begs for more. Tell him that I recognise his voice and will tell his wife!! I am lying, but caller hangs up!!

Have been told by manager that the faster I complete a call the better!!

Am upstairs trying to understand stupid behaviour regarding Tate whilst going through wardrobe for something suitable to wear for neighbour's silver wedding party at weekend when phone rings again. Pick up receiver and warn caller that I will report him to police if he doesn't get off line. Then realise that caller is own husband and not vile heavy breather.

He is breathing heavily, though, when he asks if any post has arrived for him.

Have a momentary pang of guilt over use of 'borrowed' credit card and cheque handed over to building society—however, sternly remind myself of all grievances against spouse and quickly tot up bill.

As final test I humbly ask if it's possible for him to spare any money for son's overdraft. Explain that I am totally broke.

Husband heaves deep sad sigh and says that's impossible. Hear a lot of laughing in background and ask where husband is. Says he can't tell me for security reasons, as he's being pursued for non-existent debt by malevolent nutcase. But I can hear men singing in French.

Can also hear Cheree's nasal whine as she demands to know when she is going to get the Rolex watch she has been promised!

Cross fingers and say innocently that a letter did arrive but I gave it to the nice man who called round and said he knew where to get in touch with spouse, who had forgetfully not given either me or any other potentially interested parties (bank, building society, utilities, tax authorities, etc.) a forwarding address. I also point out that I have no telephone number to reach husband in case of emergencies!

Husband seems to be having problems breathing.

Solicitously suggest he might be overdoing things, and hang up before am overwhelmed by a fit of conscience and admit morally fraudulent conversion of funds to pay off mortgage!

As I put phone down suddenly realise how many pro-active actions I am currently taking as instructed by life-coach. Sit down at computer and start to make list of current achievements.

Start adding things I would still like to achieve!

- Go to neighbour's silver wedding looking thirty-five and not fifty-one!
- Tell daughter she is better off without Brian and she should get a life!
- Have meaningful relationship with Tate
- Have raunchy sex fest with Tate
- Buy inline skates and learn to use
- Find hairdresser who understands both hair and deep-seated yearning for hairstyle that transforms current day-glo yellow rats' tails into super-sexy tousled halo that makes me look so gorgeous that no one will look at the rest of me

Okay, so am totally outside the realms of reality now, but it is, after all, a private wish list, and biggest fantasy of all on it is making it with Tate!!

Scan list and print copy. Then decide to delete

all silly references to Tate. But as I am about to do so phone rings.

It's Jacki with date for Botox party. I am not sure I really want to go to it, but Jacki refuses to take no for an answer, so I say I will go if she will help me find an outfit for silver wedding party. Also say that I cannot afford to spend more than £20! Refuse to listen to frantic objections and point out smugly that Jacki is always saying how much she likes a challenge—the harder the better!

Jacki retaliates by wailing yes, but she was referring to men when she made that comment!

Get dog and lead and decide to walk to local shops—not many left in High Street now, on account of out of town supermarkets, but current desire for organic food has led to phoenix effect at greengrocers and butchers, who both swear to sell only organic naturally produced goods from approved local suppliers.

Am not so sure about this, as have seen greengrocer down at allotments buying up excess stock of local pensioner growers, and happen to know that most maintain ruthless battle against weeds and bugs with secretly hoarded stores of DDT left over from the War!

Tie dog up outside post office and walk to butchers. Tonight it's my turn to cook and I have decided to make traditional steak and ale pie.

Have to struggle past at least half a dozen abandoned three-wheeler trendy children's buggies parked outside butchers! I glance inside at occupants. Why are all babies wearing headsets?

I ask a woman with bare midriff. She explains with a bored toss of pale blonde locks that babies are being educated by listening to tapes that will improve their intelligence. She adds smugly that her child is already on Proust.

Am speechless!!!

In butchers have to wait whilst woman in front insists on knowing pedigree of piece of lamb right down to details of animal's great-grandparents.

She eventually leaves with half a dozen free-range eggs but no meat.

Butcher red-faced with bushy eyebrows and is banging cleaver down onto slab.

Like any conscientious pet-owner, I attempt to sort out dog's needs first and request free bones for same.

Big mistake!! Butcher's face even redder and he announces in loud voice so that queue behind can hear that he has had enough of women like me trying to get something for nothing by pretending that they own a dog when they do not.

I protest that I do, and go to door to point out animal in question, but dog has gone!!

In view of busy road, and dog's predilection for male buttocks, I panic and leave shop without either meat or bones, frantically scanning surroundings for signs of carnage and blood, both animal and human. Then suddenly spot dog sitting outside door of local pet shop.

Frantically hurry over and grab what is left of chewed lead. Out of corner of my eye I suddenly realise that inside the shop is the couple with Floor Mop.

Sheba meanwhile is panting heavily and glassy-eyed, refusing to be dragged away from door, and whining pathetically.

My heart sinks. Surely dog cannot be in love with Floor Mop as she has had operation. I know from friend of friend who had everything removed by mistake when she was only going in for an x-ray that op results in total destruction of sex drive!!

I take dog home and then catch bus to super-market to buy food.

Get back just in time to be picked up by Jacki for girly shopping afternoon.

Am surprised to discover Jacki wearing strange collection of weird clothes and woolly hat pulled down over eyes.

She explains disguise is a necessary precaution as she doesn't want to be recognised.

Ends up taking me to unfamiliar part of city where apparently there is wonderful weekday market full of fabulous bargains. One slight problem! Car has to be parked over a mile away for safety!

Still, the walk will help tighten up flabby muscles!!

Hadn't realised that market is actually stalls full of rubbish—but Jacki most emphatic that am wrong and that they are actually potentially valuable soon to be v. rare antiques. Personally cannot see how tatty old velour-covered three-piece suites can ever be valuable, but bow to Jacki's superior wisdom as I know that she furnished her own fabulous riverside apartment for next to nothing—well, of course she did have to pay the buyer-cum-interior-designer £50,000 to interpret Jacki's incredibly trendy and ground-breaking ideas into reality, but that's nothing to get such a distinctive and personalised look!!

The clothes stalls are full of plastic bin liners full of clothes—am riveted at one stall where am sure have just seen a full red skirt with big white spots that I wore when I was fourteen!!

Jacki opens a bag and puts on protective surgical gloves, then dives into rubbish mountain.

Finally she emerges with a triumphant shout and waves item of clothing in front of me, announcing that it will be perfect for silver wedding and any other special event.

Am speechless. Does Jacki seriously expect me to go out wearing an old wedding dress that has been dyed bright orange?

She announces crossly that orange is the 'in' colour, karma and colour-therapy wise, and that I should be applauding her helpfulness instead of raising nit-picking objections.

Feel guilty, but, remembering I am now pro-active person who freely expresses own views, point out that orange is not a good colour on someone with my complexion.

Forget that Jacki has been into pro-active behaviour for longer than me. She sweetly points out that I am being silly as the dress almost exactly matches colour of hair!

Fortunately, before further insults can be traded, situation is resolved by another bargain-hunter snatching dress and saying it is exactly the colour she wants for her garden shed.

Four hours later—am exhausted, but Jacki refuses to admit defeat. Then we see it! Simple black linen dress in wonderful A-line style with scooped neck and bit of sleeve, and in the right size, with gorgeous tan belt next to it. Grab hold of both and throw down twenty-pound note, as stall has sign up 'Everything £10', and demand to return to car immediately before we pass out with exhaustion.

Have reached end of market when suddenly hear unearthly wail. Glancing over shoulder, see woman standing next to stall in bra and knickers demanding to know what has happened to her designer dress!! Feel for her, and tell Jacki never to bring me anywhere near market again!

Have v. pleasant evening with lodger, eating steak and ale pie and then playing cards to see who will make up next scenario for sex line caller.

He wins, and when phone rings I tell caller he must take off all his clothes and lie down with his eyes closed in his own front garden otherwise I will punish him.

Call ends abruptly when I hear a scream and then the sound of high pressure water!!

Georgie rings sounding v. excited as they now have three-dimensional scan pics of baby to show off—apparently new procedure is v. expensive, but according to both besotted parents-to-be well worth huge expenditure.

Officially baby is a boy. Erica comes on the line and confides in giggle that it is very, very definitely a boy, and looks as if he's going to be big boy as well!!

Apparently nursery is now going to be decorated in macho colours and images, as befits future superior male.

I am slightly confused by this announcement, in view of earlier comments about bringing up baby without gender differentiating, but resolve not to mention it.

Georgie is convinced that baby will be a future world-leader, Erica says he will probably be a top sportsman. Both continue to coo ecstatically until they remember that it's past ten o'clock and baby needs sleep!! They ring off after promising to come round with scan pics and asking if everything is working out with Daniel. They ask if I'm ready yet for another lodger.

I assure them that they have found me a perfect lodger in Daniel and explain that daughter due to return home at weekend so will take a rain-check on second lodger for now.

Of course secretly have plans involving daughter and Daniel. Can't think of more desirable son-in-law and father of grandchildren, but am keeping machiavellian mother hen planning to myself for time being!

Fortunately daughter is a woolly-headed idealist ripe for being leaned on by pro-active mother, and is also v. pretty!!!

CHAPTER EIGHT

HAVE switched on computer to discover ten e-mails from BB, ex-school pash, of highly explicit nature, and one from my mother, even more explicit in explaining reasons why she is divorcing current husband.

Whilst I am thinking that from content of e-mail Mother would be ideal candidate for my job I receive a second one from her announcing that she is coming to visit me. Her inner maternal voice and the runes have foretold of a crisis in my life which requires motherly intervention.

Feebly I wonder if it's possible to declare my house a plague site, to prevent mother's arrival. Still have haunting and traumatic memories of mother's previous interventions in my life, like the time she insisted on telling Derek about the importance of clitoral stimulation. This advice was passed on to him after our second date—in the middle of the High Street.

Derek was accompanied by his grandmother at the time, and the whole incident was highly embarrassing. Fortunately, as it turned out, Derek was unaware of just what a clitoris was at the time (and for a long time afterwards).

Also can never forget my mother's insisting on casting a spell on me when I went into labour with my daughter. It was supposed to ease pain in a natural healthy way, but in the ensuing argument between mother and midwife I was left on my own with contractions and no gas and air for nearly an hour, whilst mother and midwife battled it out.

Thankfully in the end the midwife was alerted to the situation by the cries of newly born daughter, although I have never understood why they couldn't hear *my* tortured screams!

Visit hospital to see old Mr Russell, who is about to be discharged. He recovered from food poisoning but unfortunately suffered a setback which increased original length of stay when he was mistaken by elderly woman in shared ward for hated ex-husband.

Luckily visitor to another patient realised something was wrong and tried to summon help—but unfortunately no nurses available. In the end, thinking Mr Russell was attacking the elderly woman, and not other way round, the helpful visitor put Mr Russell in on armlock, thus enabling elderly patient to black both Mr Russell's eyes whilst armlock unhappily broke his arm.

However, he's fine now, so I am going to see him and make arrangements to repatriate fridge-raider with rightful owner.

Although I will miss the beast, I will not miss ongoing canine sulks brought about by my refusal to go anywhere near pet shop and Sheba's love object.

Arrive at hospital to find Mr Russell's son and daughter-in-law already there. Son explains that have had family conflab and Mr Russell is now to live with them as he has developed phobic fear of elderly women.

Just one small problem! Daughter-in-law will not have dog. Daughter-in-law's mother allergic to anything with fur (apparently including husband, but that, according to Mr Russell's son, is another story), and, since mother has weak heart and strong bank balance, naturally son and wife do not wish to upset her!

I am totally sympathetic until son announces that they will arrange to have dog taken to vet's to have life humanely ended, since her uncertain temperament and large appetite means it will not be easy to find her a new home. It's the only alternative son explains, unless...

Am now officially owner of Sheba. Fortuitously Mr Russell's son had pedigree to hand, along with vaccination certificates etc. I discover that Sheba was born in May and is Taurean, which no doubt explains mega-stubborn streak, but dismiss this as am still basking in glow of being praised as wonderfully kind, generous person, as I always privately knew myself to be, despite husband claiming the complete opposite.

Daughter-in-law of Mr Russell—pretty brunette with silky sleek hair—announces that she is hairdresser and as thank-you she will do my hair for free.

Heart sinks. Experience shows that it's very unlikely that own hair will turn out looking anything other than abysmal, but Francine—the name of Mr Russell's daughter-in-law—is insistent, and somehow agree to have hair done this afternoon at home.

Before leaving hospital Mr Russell presents me with large grey tee shirt bearing words 'Remember a dog is just for Saturday night and not for life'—apparently tee shirt was gift to Mr R from grandson, but he now wants me to have it as his thank-you.

I feel somehow that Mr R has not fully taken on board the true message on tee shirt, and have to avoid son's eyes as I thank him for it.

Return home to prepare bedroom for daughter's arrival at weekend and own nervous system in anticipation of new hairstyle.

There's a stern message on telephone from sex

line manager ordering me to report for re-training as I have been receiving complaints!!! Resolve to do better!

Francine arrives and determinedly sets to work. Am terrified. Dog has been banned from house in case Francine's mother detects any canine smell on her return. Dreadful pathetic whinging filling kitchen—think at first it's banished dog, then realise it is me!!

Two hours later am now a convert to the existence of miracles. Have spent hour since Francine's departure staring at own reflection in mirror.

Francine has transformed ugly orange disaster into gleaming trendily brown and blonde hairstyle like those worn by sexy TV presenters. Meg Ryan eat your heart out!!!

Am totally besotted with new image, and resolve to follow Francine's advice and throw out frosted blue eyeshadow have been wearing ever since Derek commented on our engagement night that it made my eyes look sexy—also pale pink muted lipstick that clashes with my complexion.

Instead am to buy new foundation, taupe eyeshadow and new lipstick—Francine has written down colours and makes for me. Has also suggested she will come and keep a close eye on progress of new hairstyle—for free. Think about asking if she is feeling generous and grateful enough to trim dog's hair also, but decide against it. After all, there is her mother's allergy to think about. Also it isn't ever a good idea to have two attractive females in same household!!

Dog shows appreciation of new look me by throwing up dinner on living room carpet. Discover when cleaning up mess that she has been in rubbish, eating stuff that's past its sell-by date. No wonder she's sick. Have learned from doggie-type book I just happened to purchase on way back from hospital that Alsations (sorry, Sheba— German Shepherds) have very delicate stomachs— plus cannily high intelligence. This could explain gleam in dog's eye as she watches me clean up mess.

Later still—Daniel comes in and admires my new hairstyle without having to be told and insists I give a twirl to show it off. He grins and says it's v. sexy and that should show SNN just what he's missing.

When I look mortified he explains that he over-heard me talk to myself about silly crush!!

Am more and more convinced that Daniel will make daughter a wonderful husband and me an equally wonderful son-in-law. He's almost too much of a sweetie!!

I swear him to secrecy, and admit that am ridic-ulously fathoms deep in desire for handsome neighbour. I sigh and say that I know he does not share my feelings, but Daniel disagrees. Says that from man's point of view he can detect definite signs of interest from SNN. Want to believe him but suspect he is just trying to be kind.

Change subject by showing him tee shirt! Both laugh whilst Sheba gives baleful look. Take opportunity to explain to him about impending arrival of mother and her odd habits. He says not to worry; his own grandmother was seventh child of seventh child and has decamped to Delphi in Greece as she thinks she is reincarnation of original oracle worker—adds that it was timely departure as neighbours had begun to complain about weeds she was allowing to grow in her garden.

'Weed' being the right description, Daniel further confides. He explains that grandmother denies that she was growing stuff for recreational use but merely for medicinal purposes.

I confide to him about my own pathetic and miserable lack of any drug-taking experience, and about *Cosmo* list. Also feel forced to be honest and admit that am not truly comfortable with modern ethos on subject of drug-taking. Daniel responds that drugs not his scene either, and that he does not consider them to be in any way cool.

Now am tempted to lock Daniel away in room so no other mother with marriageable daughter can get sight of him until have him safely married to own daughter!!!

Am of course doing my best in that direction by dropping hints about daughter's virtues and beauty!

Spend rest of evening playing Scrabble for rude words and then cards. Discover at end of night have lost Scrabble but have won ten pounds!! Good! Will go towards new make-up.

Today is the day of silver wedding party and of own private plan to stun Tate with wonderful new appearance—like butterfly emerging from chrysalis, like phoenix rising from ashes...like...like middle-aged woman making total fool of herself?

Ignore own critical self-doubting voice and go out and buy new make-up—insist that startled salesgirl shows me how to make eyes look like hers—but without the diamante-studded eyeliner. After all, it's a daytime do and I don't want to look as though I'm trying too hard!!

I go home and prepare bedroom for daughter. Daniel is in her old room, as it has own *en suite* bathroom, so she will have to make do with her brother's room for now. Am in middle of preparing other bedrooms for redecorating.

Sheba still v. quiet and sulky. Refuses to go for walk and pointedly ignores dinner.

Feel bad and decide since it's an afternoon party I will take her with me.

Go upstairs to get ready. Have butterflies in tummy and hand is shaking so much have to make four attempts to get eyeshadow on eyes. But at last am ready! New dress looks terrific—pity, of course, about small accident with expensive new fake tan treatment I allowed salesgirl to persuade me into buying, but fortunately have managed to cover up worst of streaks and untanned patches with make-up.

Can't wear tights as am wearing open-toed high-heeled sandals (aka 'Shagging Shoes', according to Jacki) which, strictly speaking, belong to Cheree. I found them with heels stuck into soft ceiling of car over back seat before Derek robbed the vehicle.

They are a little on large size, so will have to walk v. carefully in them.

Have painted toenails with new polish and have remembered that perfume should be sprayed wherever a person wants to be kissed!!

Have almost emptied bottle before I realise what I am doing!!!

Totter downstairs and go into kitchen to collect silver wedding present (bottle of wine) and dog. Find dog skulking in corner chewing something grey.

Discover something grey is, or rather was, new tee shirt. I'm sure I can see triumphant look in dog's eyes when I realise she has ripped off message!!

Almost decide against taking her to the party, but kind-hearted streak overwhelms common sense.

Daniel has offered to drive me to party—it's only down road, but in view of instability in borrowed shoes I thankfully accept.

I am just struggling to get out of bucket seat of Daniel's sports car when I see Tate approaching with goddaughter.

Goddaughter squeals when Sheba bounds up to Tate, grimacing in horror as dog rubs herself against his immaculate clothes.

As I apologise I realise Tate is giving me a v. cool look. Immediately feel mortified and v. low. He must have guessed my silly feelings and is also probably remembering unedifying sight of naked boobs and comparing same to taut unfettered projections perched on chest of goddaughter. Can't understand why Daniel should think Tate is interested in me when it's obvious he's not!!

It's obvious too that Tate is not drawn to Daniel, as he's regarding him with ferocious expression. I wonder why, specially when Daniel is being so helpful and kind, even kissing me reassuringly in filial way as well as being solicitously concerned for my own enjoyment of party.

Ignoring dark furrowed brows and v. excitingly sexy look Tate is giving me, I head for neighbour's garden, trying to look elegant—not easy when attached to large dog and wearing high heels!!

Everyone at party is kind and seems to know about situation re Derek, but cannot help feeling forlorn as I watch neighbours with partners. Even nosy neighbour from three up is clutching arm of own husband, despite complaining about him to me.

I can remember quite clearly my own silver wedding celebration—after all, it was only two years ago.

And I still have a bit of a green mark on my arm from bracelets Derek gave me. Have a vivid memory of how angry he was about it. Blamed me totally for having 'funny skin'. I can understand that he must have felt disappointed after spending so long searching for present—turned out he had bought them whilst on holiday—sorry, business trip—with Cheree—although he only told me that when he announced that he was leaving.

Still have silver plants in garden, and other presents given by friends. Suddenly feel very alone and sorry for self. Everyone else seems to be part of a pair, and it doesn't help that I can plainly see Tate, with goddaughter clinging to his arm, surrounded by a small admiring crowd.

Suddenly realise am being stared at with fixed concentration by a woman standing several yards away.

Wonder feverishly if she is someone I know, as face vaguely familiar. Woman is wearing obviously expensive and enviable cream silk trouser suit and menacing frown. Comes over and admires dress. Says she had one exactly the same—an exclusive designer number bought in Milan. She states that dress was stolen from market stall whilst she was trying on antique lace bargain.

Immediately express sisterly horror and empathise, whilst my heart pounds with guilt as I remember agonised shriek I heard after purchasing dress from market stall. Suspect am about to be asked where got dress, but fortunately Sheba—wonderful dog—creates diversion before other woman can speak.

Unfortunately diversion is not so wonderful as it involves pulling so hard on lead that I almost lose balance. Decide it's easier to let go of lead than risk falling over and jeopardising my dignity—after all, dog is in secure environment, and I am already in diligent if somewhat slow pursuit of escaped hound.

Afternoon has become overcast and I can hear hostess announcing that perhaps we should make our way indoors. Caterers will remove beautifully set out and artistic buffet which cost small fortune from tables on lawn to brand-new luxury conservatory which was happy couple's silver wedding 'treat' to themselves. But am too busy hurrying after dog to pay much attention to odd spot of rain.

See dog disappear in middle of crowd of guests, followed by sharp piercing howl of terror.

Crowd parts to reveal Floor Mop and owners. To my horror Sheba has mounted Floor Mop and is vigorously humping, regardless of fact that this is not her role. Female owner of dog is screaming and interested crowd of young children have gathered to watch, whilst parents hurry protectively to cover innocent eyes from the sight of such unbridled lust.

Hear one sweet toddler lisping, 'Daddy—is it doing it doggie-style, like you keep asking Mummy?'

Red-faced parent exits to the sounds of coughs and titters, whilst equally red-faced host bears down on me and demands that I control Sheba.

Remembering timely action of sexy Tate last time, I run to buffet, grab slice of beef and show it temptingly to Sheba.

She immediately ceases humping and releases sad quivering wreck of object of ardour in favour of beef. Am about to reach for lead and apologise when dog suddenly realises where meat came from and heads in direction of buffet.

Massed ranks of catering staff manfully attempt to deflect canine assault on food as indeed does hapless dog owner, i.e. me. But suddenly Sheba gives Oscar-worthy performance of wolf in dog's clothing. It's impossible to blame catering staff for breaking ranks. Would have done same myself if I hadn't been on other end of lead as Sheba charged. Also silly to blame caterers for using fragile trestle tables. Not their fault that they collapse when Sheba places front paws on table to assault the beef.

Luckily I did manage to haul her off, but admit that was in part on account of her having seen the whole ham on bone in middle of wonderful display of delicately shaped salad vegetables and ice carving.

Hostess screams as Sheba runs under table with ham bone. I did try to help hostess remove king prawns from décolleté of her frock, but forgot I still had hold of lead and didn't realise it was twisted round leg of table.

Am not sure what would have happened if heavens hadn't suddenly opened and clouds burst into rain. In mad rush for cover crowd stampeded over collapsed part of buffet display, whilst I wrestled with Sheba over ham bone.

Could feel rain begin to soak me, but nobly ignored discomfort in determination to restore ham bone to rightful owner. However, when I finally managed to retrieve bone, and present it to hostess, hostess was too emotional to make any response. Red-faced husband v. ungratefuly insisted that I should leave, and even more humiliation was heaped on my undeserving head when I happened to look into the conservatory as I walked past and saw that Tate was standing by window with goddaughter, who was shrieking with laughter whilst pointing at me! I see that Tate is frowning and he starts to walk towards self. I go all hot and achey inside with longing, but goddaughter pulls him back.

I give them both a haughtily dismissive look, but then happen to look down at body and realise that carefully applied make-up has run to reveal inexpert application of fake tan, which for some reason has how developed unappealing greenish tinge!!

Creep home with tail between legs—unlike dog, who is extremely jaunty. Beast has no sense of shame—or gratitude. As I her rub fur dry with a towel in the kitchen I point out huffily that but for me she would be on the mantelpiece in an urn by now!

Dog gives me look of melting devotion and tenderly removes itinerant flea from arm.

Am moved to tears.

I have a bath, put on dressing gown, and relate whole unhappy incident to Daniel over a cup of tea.

Am just admitting genuine mistake over acquisition of dress when doorbell rings.

Assuming it's arrival of daughter, go to answer. Only not daughter standing on doorstep but Tate!!!

Am sure I can hear heavenly choir singing!!!

As I stare at Tate, unable to drag gaze away from gorgeous sexy eyes, realise that he has come so close to me that I can feel heat coming off his gorgeous lustable body.

Feel I could easily swoon, just like real Georgette Heyer heroine.

Wonder why Tate has come round, and imagination runs riot as I fantasise about him sweeping me up into strong, masculine arms and announcing that he cannot live without me any longer…that he loves me to distraction…that he thinks me most wonderful woman on earth…that he wants to marry me immediately!!

Am just about to accept wonderful marriage proposal when I hear Tate explaining that he was passing and thought he would call and see how I was doing with the achievements list.

Am struggling womanfully with mega disappointment and heartbreak when Sheba, having heard Tate's voice, emerges from kitchen to give him soulful look.

Just about to suggest that we go into the kitchen so I can describe progress of wish list in detail (anything to keep him in same room as me as in truth there isn't any progress to describe), when Daniel suddenly emerges from sitting room, unaware of Tate's presence, and announces he is going to make special supper for us both.

Hall suddenly feels as though central heating has gone off and winter chill descended. Tate says that he's sorry to have intruded and that he could not stay anyway as he's taking goddaughter out to dinner as compensation for missing out on the buffet Sheba destroyed.

He has gone before I can think of anything to say.

Am wallowing in self-pity and despair, picturing Tate having dinner with gorgeous younger woman, when doorbell rings again. Hopes rise, but it's not Tate.

This time it's daughter.

Although affected by traumatic events of the day—especially Tate leaving—I do make a bit of an effort to welcome daughter warmly with motherly hug, and am hurt when daughter recoils from maternal embrace with look of irritation on face.

Try to tell daughter about Daniel, who I am anxious for her to meet so that they can fall in love with one another and start making me beautiful grandchildren, but daughter refuses to listen. Disapprovingly, she demands to know how come she hadn't heard before that a man is living under my roof! I tell daughter how attractive Daniel is, and how he has filled lonely gap in my life, not to mention that he's a wonderful cook!

Am shocked by the ferocity of daughter's angry glare at me.

Strange how I never noticed before how much daughter looks like Derek's mother at times.

Turning her back on me, daughter marches into living room where dog is now lying on her back chewing a toy.

I start to introduce Daniel to daughter, but daughter totally ignores introduction and says that she is shocked and disgusted with me, and that Daniel is a despicable slimeball from gutter and should return there. She also states that dog is unhygienic, before sweeping out and going upstairs.

I hear a door opening upstairs and realise that daughter has gone into Daniel's room, thinking it's still hers! However, before I can say anything, phone rings. It is pervy heavy breather, wanting to know what I am wearing and if have a friend who wants to join in fun session!!

I say I have a perfect partner for him, especially if he likes it doggie-style, and am just beginning to enjoy myself describing Sheba's winsome feminine attributes, including habit of sinking fangs into neck of love object, when I hear a loud scream from upstairs followed by crash.

I put down receiver whilst perv is in mid-groan and go upstairs.

Door to Daniel's room is open. Daniel is standing inside, covered in compost from spider plant that was in *en suite* bathroom, surrounded by bits of broken pot and leaves whilst daughter is standing stark naked on bedroom carpet with red face.

After much shouting and screaming discover that daughter had gone into supposedly own bedroom to shower and that Daniel, not realising she was there, had gone into bedroom to give me time to calm daughter down.

In the end, since neither daughter nor Daniel listen to my explanations, I leave room—having told daughter she is sleeping in son's bedroom.

Dog is in v. funny mood… She has stolen old teddy bear of son's and is sleeping with it, refusing to let anyone else get near her. I resolve to consult vet. Understand dog might be frustrated—must be if she fancies Floor Mop—and I can certainly relate to her feelings—but she has to learn to be more mature and to recognise value of self-denial.

Just like I am having to do over unrequited love for Tate!

Go to bed and have confused dream in which I am under buffet table with Tate...

CHAPTER NINE

AM NOW in hiding from and have been sent to Coventry by virtually all of my neighbours. Sheba escaped yesterday and had to be retrieved from outside pet shop, where she was lying in wait for Floor Mop.

Have been told by hostess of silver wedding party that I am a disgrace to the neighbourhood and I am lowering whole tone of area. Apparently they were prepared to turn a blind eye to my moving in a younger lover, but stealing the rich cousin's dress from a market stall and then flaunting it at a party, and allowing dog to behave in v. indelicate way in front of innocent young children was TOO MUCH, not to mention destruction of buffet and ruining of whole event.

I try to apologise, but I am interrupted by daughter coming downstairs, demanding to know why Daniel is sleeping in her room instead of mine.

Heart sinks as neighbour makes a speedy exit before I can explain true meaning of daughter's inflammatory statement.

I discover from daughter, as she rummages in fridge wanting to know why I have not stocked up on healthy vegetarian food for her, that she is refusing to give up her own room and bed. I discover also that because of this, she spent night sleeping in same bed as Daniel, who also refused to give up his own sleeping accommodation.

Discussion comes to a halt when dog bares teeth at daughter. Quickly explain that dog is undergoing traumatic sexual identity crisis and is reluctant to admit another female to the household. Dog and daughter eye one another balefully.

I assure daughter that problem is soon to be resolved when I take dog to vet for check-up.

To prove point, I ring the number on papers handed over to me by Mr Russell. However, as soon as I mention dog's pedigree name, and that of Mr Russell, the receptionist drops the receiver.

Several seconds later vet comes on the phone and explains that Sheba is banned from surgery for unsocial canine behaviour. When I demand to know what this was, am told coldly that dog attempted to sexually abuse young male trainee veterinary nurse when she was being prepared for operation. Humbly I ask if vet can provide name of a doggy psychiatrist, and am given some details of one that charges £70 per hour. Vet replaces receiver whilst I am still trying to recover from shock.

Daughter and Daniel are totally refusing to speak to one another, but incredibly are sleeping together as both refuse to give up bed. I will never understand modern generation!!! If I was sharing bed with Tate last thing on my mind would be sleep!!!!

Tonight I am going to Jacki's Botox party, and decide to wear new linen dress again.

Francine comes to do my hair, and we talk about the state of geriatric wards in hospitals. Decide that if I ever win lottery I will make big donation towards new state-of-art ward for proper care for elderly. This is not totally altruistic as I will be needing it myself soon... Sooner if daughter and Daniel keep up current level of hostility.

I am picked up by Rosie to go to Botox party. She says that final arrangements are in hand for Schooldays-r-Us reunion and that it has been decided everyone will go in school uniform and food is to be genuine school dinners.

Arrive at party to discover I am something of a celebrity on account of article in newspaper.

Discover later that Jacki has told other invitees that I have already had Botox, which explains why I now miraculously look closer to fifty-five than seventy-five of newspaper photograph!! Discover also that as supposed old hand on Botox scene, I am to be lucky recipient of trainee beauty therapist's attempt to show efficacy of treatment.

Sit so stiffly that whole body might have already been injected as therapist explains that, since normally Botox takes three to ten days to work, to make sure that everyone can see how effective the treatment is, she will give me double normal amount!!

I try to object and escape, but as Jacki has cleverly tied me up in borrowed dentist's chair, which she now tilts back, it is impossible!

Therapist further sweetly explains that it is impossible to add any kind of numbing anaesthetic agent to Botox, and so teeny-weeny pricks may hurt just a little bit!!!

OWW!

Friends, she lied. Teeny-weeny pricks were big hard jabs and hurt like hell…

Jacki complained that my screams drowned out lovely soothing mood music on CD player and caused next door neighbour to ring police and say that someone was being murdered.

Fortunately police too busy to respond to call, although Jacki did say later that they came round next day.

Whilst I am being fortified after ordeal with glass of wine overhear two women discussing gorgeous sexy American man who has moved into area.

'Yes, he is gorgeous,' one of pair agrees with other. 'But don't bother wasting your time—after all, darling, at our time of life—haven't got it to waste, have we? The sexy man is already spoken for. He has a live-in girlfriend. A young, tall, blonde!!! I saw them locked in a passionate embrace yesterday morning when I drove past.'

Immediately realise the pair are talking about Tate and seethe inwardly with jealousy as I recognise supposed goddaughter in description of girlfriend. Hate Tate for lying, and hate myself even more for being fool enough to believe him!!

Everyone is now admiring my immobilised features, whilst Jacki urges friends to make immediate bookings for treatment.

Beauty therapist hovers over me and says it's a pity about deep ugly grooves alongside mouth, but they can easily be fixed with quick injection of filler. I tremble whilst Jacki enthusiastically urges therapist to show the gathered throng how effective treatment is. I want to go home, but am still trapped in chair.

This time is not as painful but probably because I am concentrating on pain caused by collapse of foolish dreams over Tate.

I am not allowed to see own reflection until therapist is finished, but when I get a glimpse I am totally lost for words.

Forehead is covered in red dots and is now grotesquely swollen, whilst blood is dripping from pinpricks inflicted on sides of mouth.

Therapist is gaily suggesting she could drain unpleasant red veins on nose, but announce that I don't want to be selfish and it's only fair that someone else should benefit from her expertise. Am about to volunteer Jacki when I realise I still have to be released from chair!!

Decide to walk home, as I need fresh air, and am just turning into road when I see Tate walking towards me.

I immediately cross the road to avoid having to acknowledge presence of lying heartbreaker who is probably secretly laughing at my gullibility whilst enjoying sexy young body of supposed 'goddaughter'.

Nearly trip on cracked paving slab and just manage to suppress scream of pain from possibly broken big toe.

Spend rest of walk home mentally planning letter I will write to council about disgraceful state of pavements whilst they extort money from householders for their maintenance, but then remember that one of my unpaid bills is for Council Tax, so regretfully abandon mental rant.

Get home to find dog, daughter and Daniel occupying kitchen in mutual silent hostility.

Take dog for walk and call at chip shop on way back. Conceal evidence of secretive meal in skip outside Tate's house, and notice as I am doing so a photograph of Tate looking sexily stern in frame.

Discover that frame is wedged in rubbish, but soon manage to release it by climbing into skip and pushing rubbish to one side.

Clamber back to pavement, clutching object of desire, which I immediately conceal beneath coat. If can't have the man then I can at least have the photograph to dream over!!

As I look round with furtive manner of experienced criminal I realise that there is black object protruding from nosy neighbour's bedroom window.

Scuttle home, hoping skip rummage has not been witnessed!!

Daughter is now missing from kitchen. She has not taken up occupancy of bed—as I had thought—but has left a note to say she has gone out to an all-night supermarket to buy food!!

Agree with Daniel that daughter is difficult, and that there's no reason why she should not occupy brother's bedroom. Offer to halve rent to make up for intransigence, but thankfully Daniel refuses.

I am in sitting room 'working'—describing in explicit and unwholesome detail a sexual act to caller who I am sure is golf club president—when daughter returns.

I finish the call and go into kitchen to be confronted by red-faced and red-eyed virago of daughter claiming that I am a disgusting pervert and that she is ashamed that I am her mother!!

She says she blames Daniel totally for my corruption and that she is going to write to the authorities at the university, and to the building society, revealing unlawful letting of her bedroom and disgusting behaviour of me and Daniel.

I am about to respond when kitchen door opens and Daniel comes in. Daughter immediately launches into diatribe too complicated and long-winded to go into here. Suffice it to say that daughter feels defiled by having to breathe same air as us.

Fortunately she has to and, whilst she takes a gulp of it, I quickly explain that I was not talking to Daniel in sitting room but to a 'client'.

Daughter goes white and sinks to floor, but is thankfully prevented from damaging me by being clutched by Daniel.

When daughter is restored to full consciousness, she weakly pleads to be told that I am joking and that her mother has not turned to life of sin and vice of type too horrible to contemplate.

I vigorously defend my morals and explain necessity of earning a living since father has left huge debts and no money. Daughter is still pale and asks why I couldn't get a decent job instead of selling myself on street.

Am about to correct further misapprehension when doorbell rings. Go to answer and discover husband of nosy neighbour at three up on doorstep (him of the 'funny little ways').

Visitor clears throat and steps into hall. He explains that it is his duty as self-appointed Neighbourhood Watch person to keep our road free of crime. This involves exhausting night and day vigilance, which is why he has taken to videoing the road and all goings on in it.

He says he knows from his wife that I am having a hard time, but he hadn't realised it was so hard that I had been reduced to searching neighbours' rubbish.

He clears his throat again, and puts a cold, clammy hand on my arm. He says that he is willing to help and is sure we could come to mutually agreeable arrangement. Before I can speak, he says eagerly that he has always admired me and it would only involve posing for him for 'artistic' photographs he is keen to take. Adds that he already has all the necessary props and has remote-controlled video for special effects. Is just starting to explain to me about his wife not understanding him when daughter bursts into hall and announces that she will call police unless he leaves immediately!

Dog joins the fray and sinks teeth into his skinny behind as he scuttles out of the door.

In ensuing heated exchange I attempt to explain to daughter that I am not trawling streets selling sex, but I am actually performing necessary public service. Yes, all right, I had thought I would be working in a call centre, soothing irate customers accusing utility companies of driving them mad with canned Handel water torture music, instead of allowing them to complain about the grossly inflated bills. But it was a simple error that anyone could make, and I am only trying to do my best and keep roof over our heads.

Daughter retires to bed still refusing to believe that I am not having rabid affair with Daniel, and is apparently still determined to sleep in his bed to prevent him sleeping in mine!!!

Pour myself a glass of wine and retire to bedroom to inspect suddenly seriously arched eyebrows and permanently surprised expression!

CHAPTER TEN

TODAY am due to collect mother from airport. Daniel has generously volunteered to act as chauffeur since although daughter has a car she has flatly refused to do anything to help.

I remember that daughter and mother never really hit it off, but it is not my fault both invited themselves to stay with me at the same time.

Mother is to have newly decorated bedroom which I have finally finished painting. Am pleased with effect, although paint is not exactly colour shown on chart. Should have been palest apple-green—is more like dark toad. But that should suit mother!

Mother's flight due in at midnight. At one o'clock I am prowling round now empty arrivals lounge worrying as only mature daughter of eccentric elderly mother can.

At last I hear voices and laughter, and the flight crew—all male—arrive in hall. In middle of group is enviably skinny blonde in low-rise jeans exposing flat belly with diamond-studded belly button and tiny crop top barely covering firm taut boobs.

Vision is clutching silly little bag with designer logo and flight crew are carrying huge mound of designer luggage.

I ignore the group and then have sudden rush of blood to head as I recognise a voice! The blonde is mother. I do double check. Is definitely mother. Wow!

It's not true what it said in *Cosmo*. Mother could easily pass for my sister—younger sister—much younger sister…

Nudge Daniel and totter feebly over to blonde vision, who is saying something to the Captain about enjoying the view from flight deck. For some reason mother's comment provokes much male mirth, which I ignore.

I attempt to embrace mother in welcome, but she is ignoring me to flirt breathlessly with Daniel. Poor soul is quite obviously totally bemused and I suspect already besotted.

Mother is a real spellbinder! As well as spell-maker!

Daughter has waited up to greet her grandmother and announces in loud voice whilst slamming door that she is surprised American FDA has allowed mother to leave country without a health toxicity warning stamped on head.

Mother coos sweetly that she can see that daughter hasn't changed. And that she has new spell which will help!

*   *   *

Is now three days since mother arrived—feels like three lifetimes. She has announced that she was not surprised about my marriage break-up since she never felt Derek and I were suited as he was too boring.

Daughter and mother have set up opposing battle camps, and various parts of house now total no-go areas. Mother has also announced that she is leaving current husband as he's too old and boring and he has lost sex drive—he's fifty-five.

Daughter is v. unpleasant about short life of mother's marriages and hints that mother is making unfair demands.

Have introduced mother to Jacki, as I feel they have much in common. However, mother has offended Jacki by saying one can always tell a cut-price facelift and that it's as bad as wearing chain-store clothes—in fact worse, as clothes can be ditched. Mother, of course, only wears top designer ranges, but says she does make small economies such as not wearing underwear (hope she is joking).

Mother has announced that she will pay for my breast op if I want one. Daughter has retaliated by leaving photos of horribly mutilated female bodies on kitchen table and in biscuit cupboard. Has also taken to leaving long, boring articles about effect of alcohol on female liver all over place!!

Mother has filled fridge with champagne and unlabelled bottles containing strange coloured liquid.

When I enquire as to contents I am told that they are totally necessary to aid mother's current youthful face and figure. Am eager to know what the stuff is and mother confides that is her own urine. Ugh! Apparently drinking it is latest Hollywood thing and v. effective. She says I should try it but I fear I do not share mother's total dedication to the search for eternal youth—although must say I am tired of being asked who mother is and getting stunned looks of disbelief when I explain.

Mother is totally disgusted by fact that daughter is still sleeping with Daniel. She says it is a complete waste of a gorgeous sexy man and that she is sure Daniel would enjoy sleeping with her more.

Mother has also opened my own eyes with her robust and inventive responses to the suddenly increased number of sex-line callers asking for her!!

Have even received commendation from manager!!!

Daughter is v. unkind and unfair about persons living on immoral earnings until mother points out that no one is more likely to live on immoral earnings than a lawyer, which is daughter's own profession.

Mother has been using computer and has discovered unedited list created by me—including all items about Tate!

She demands to know identity of Sexy New Neighbour but I refuse to give any information. Mother retires to the sitting room in a sulk with dog, to watch television.

Am just having blissful quiet few minutes on my own in the kitchen, since daughter refuses to enter on account of (a) unhygienic presence of dog and (b) even more unhygienic presence of her grandmother's pee in fridge, when I hear daughter going into sitting room.

Suddenly hear terrible screams and howls, and rush there.

Mother has wrestled daughter to sofa and is clutching TV remote control in triumph whilst dog stands guard.

As I try to mediate between warring parties, daughter demands that wild bitch be evicted straight away. Takes me several valuable seconds to realise she is referring not to dog but to grandmother!!

Immediately remonstrate with daughter, who bursts into tears and says she has always known she was never really wanted.

Assure her that that's not true—and anyway, it's not my fault that her father told her she was the result of a burst condom!!

After daughter flounces out, turn to mother to remonstrate so that I am doling out equal punishment, but mother defends her actions by saying that daughter selfishly came in and tried to change TV channel right in middle of vitally important programme.

Look at screen to see we are in the middle of sentimental animal rescue programme and ask mother witheringly what is so vital? Have scientists discovered new breed of toad? Mother is extremely huffy and says that as a matter of fact it was not her who was watching programme but dog.

V. importantly mother announces that she hadn't intended to say anything, but she must now confide to me that she is on the brink of starting a v. profitable new career, having just undergone a fortnight's intensive training as a dog whisperer.

Am flabbergasted. When I have stopped laughing mother insists sniffily that she is serious.

In an attempt to reinstate reality, suggest that with her new skills mother can find out why dog is a sex maniac.

Am banished to sofa whilst mother switches off TV and sits on floor in front of dog.

After much stroking and eyeball-gazing mother takes deep breath and announces that dog is mortally offended by my comments and considers herself to be no such thing. Mother also says dog resents daughter switching off programme of highly sensitive nature—i.e. rescue of shamefully treated domestic pets.

I tell mother she was more convincing as witch and leave room.

This evening is Schooldays-r-Us reunion party. Since I no longer have original school uniform I have decided to wear hideous designer outfit supplied for newspaper article.

However, first am to go and see Mr Russell's daughter-in-law, who is to fix false plaits to own hair.

Mother has volunteered to walk dog. I say sweetly that that is fine by me as I'm sure they must have lots to talk about.

Whole road is agog following mistake in the newspaper naming our street as the most valuable area for potential property investment in country, as revealed per secret documents leaked by Borough Council.

Whole road now filled with limousines with blacked-out windows whilst men in suits doorstep houses making ridiculous offers to buy.

I have had three offers already this morning—I told last would-be buyer that no way would I part with treasured family home for measly £6m.

Mother has put on television so she and dog can monitor situation and be first to hear PM's plea for restraint and assurance that whole thing is a big mistake.

Am just about to go out when doorbells rings. It's nosy neighbour from three up, red-eyed and carrying huge suitcase.

When I ask politely if she going on holiday Neighbour promptly bursts into noisy tears and in-serts herself into our hallway.

She explains between sobs that her husband has told her he has sold house to entrepreneur for £10m and that she must move out.

I say waspishly that, if true, I cannot see why she should be crying. More loud sobs as nosy neighbour explains that husband rang from Concorde en route to Caribbean, where he has de-cided to relocate—without her.

She says she knows how kind and generous I am, and also that I have many spare bedrooms, so is moving in for time being until nerves are settled enough to make other arrangements!!

I return home from wonderful peace of Francine's home—she only has four children, all boys, and old Mr Russell to deal with plus husband—to find that daughter and nosy neighbour have joined ranks and are in process of conducting strip search of kitchen to remove all sources of alcoholic liquor.

Go upstairs and change into revolting party outfit, paint freckles on my face in mood of overexcited teenager that I once was, and put on new bra I have been persuaded to buy by smarmy shop assistant that is supposed to enhance cleavage and give uplift but has in fact reduced boobs to something that looks like squashed sausage stuffed into overtight skin.

Reach hallway just as front door opens and mother returns, clutching dog and arm of Tate.

Seethe with furious jealousy as mother giggles girlishly and bats unnaturally thick and healthy-looking eyelashes at my own object of lustful desire.

Turns out mother called to visit Tate having recognised fellow American whilst glancing into car and seeing copy of *Washington Post*.

Am gritting teeth too hard to remind mother that she is not American at all, and that I know for a fact she never reads anything other than celebrity magazines.

According to mother, she discovered Tate on his own feeling lonely, so insisted on bringing him home so he could share homely loving atmosphere and enjoyable family meal.

Am prevented from replying by sound of breaking glass from kitchen as anti-drink zealots reach fever-pitch.

Whilst mother and daughter and nosy neighbour are arguing about benefits and hazards of wine Daniel walks in and bursts out laughing. Suddenly remember what I am wearing!!

'Mmmm. Sexy,' Daniel teases me, tweaking plait and kissing my cheek.

Tate announces tersely that he has to leave.

I childishly toss plaits and hear self saying, 'Of course. I expect you're meeting your *goddaughter*.'

I tense as Tate turns round and gives me cool look from amazing sexy eyes. Feel cheap and mean and want to burst into tears.

'No, as a matter of fact I'm not,' he replies.

Phone rings and mother answers. Hear her call out, 'Kitty, it's for you—one of your pervy clients.'

Thanks mother!

Oh, to be able to faint at will, like a Regency heroine!!!

Reunion party is being held in local scout hut as it was the only place committee could afford.

I arrive with Jacki and Rosie to find party in full swing. Take paper cup full of lemonade that I am offered as I walk in and gulp as I am thirsty. I feel as though my throat is on fire and almost spit it out!

Jacki then reminds me that we always used to refer to vodka as lemonade when we were at school, so as to disguise under-age drinking from teachers.

Remember that she did, but I certainly did not, since I have never had a good head for alcohol. Might enjoy odd glass of healthy red wine, but never touch spirits. Have done now, in error, and am beginning to feel distinctly unwell!!

On account of stinginess of attendees, plans to serve replica school dinner have been axed, and room reverberates to sound of sixties music. Am sure I can actually smell scent of chalk and sweaty flannel trousers as study excited eager faces of ex-schoolmates.

In order to save embarrassment and time all attendees have been issued with name tag bearing nickname of choice. Own simply reads 'DGT'. I furtively look around for sexy e-mail sender. Have discreetly hinted to Jacki and Rosie about nature of correspondence received from most desirable boy in school, and must be honest have basked a little in their reaction. However, I didn't think it very kind of Jacki to claim that sexy co-student never told her that he had undying pash for me, but then from what she remembers of him, he would have shagged anything that moved!!

Manage to make way through crowd to find table and sit down. Jacki is already looking for new recruits for Botox party and cosmetic surgery trip, whilst Rosie is on third glass of 'lemonade'.

Search crowd discreetly, looking for my admirer. (Have secretly and cleverly sent him e-mail describing my outfit and reminding admirer of his lust for me in school socks and short skirt.) No, of course I can never feel about admirer the way I do about Tate, but then admirer is available and Tate is not!! Which reminds me. I must tell mother that Tate is not available and that urine is no substitute for twenty-something hormones and own teeth.

I am suddenly aware of hot breath on the back of my neck and I turn round, recoiling in horror as I see snotty-nosed wimp from one year below mine. Odd how he hasn't changed at all. But then to be fair he was almost bald at school.

He is staring at my badge and as I stare haughtily back I suddenly realise that badge snotty-nose is wearing reads 'BB'.

The same feeling that attacked me when I hadn't done my homework spreads through my insides in odiously familiar way as unwelcome truth dawns.

It is not sexiest stud in school who has been e-mailing me with pornographic suggestions but snotty-nosed wimp!!

Decide I will have to plead headache if am to escape derision of Jacki and Rosie, but before I can say anything snotty-nosed wimp suddenly bursts out in high-pitched complaint that I am attending do under false pretences and I am not the love of his life, even though I'm wearing badge with letters of her nickname—i.e. 'Dull, Grumpy Tart'.

An ugly scene is only just averted by quick thinking of Jacki and Rosie, who rise magnificently to occasion and give wimp Chinese burn whilst pouring vodka down his throat, threatening to reveal that his badge of 'BB' stands for 'Big Baby'!!

End up having fun-filled evening reminiscing about old times and maths teacher with predilection for bare bottoms and rulers, until I discover that one of group round the table is maths teacher's niece. She is not offended, though, and says she now understands why mother banned uncle from house.

Get Rosie to drop me off at end of road on way home. Claim that I need fresh air to clear head and remove smell of alcohol before going home, but sad truth is that am consumed by need to walk past Tate's house.

The house is in darkness as I start to walk past, wondering jealously if Tate is already in bed with sexy supposed goddaughter. Tate obviously oblivious to emotional pain and misery he is causing me. I start to cry and then feel sick. Wish I had not drunk lemonade-vodka by mistake as now feel v. odd indeed!

I am sitting beside pond in Tate's front garden, having earnest discussion with fishing garden gnome about LIFE, when front door to house opens and I see Tate striding toward me.

Try to stand up, but I am too dizzy. No doubt it's another menopausal symptom I am being forced to suffer by malevolent Mother Nature. Try to explain to Tate that I am in middle of deep meaningful discussion with gnome, but Tate has hand on arm and am unable to make quivering vocal chords do anything other than moan. In fact whole body is quivering.

Am inside Tate's house!! With Tate!! Am ecstatic and on total high of joyous abandonment as is only natural when in presence of deeply beloved and desired male sex object.

That I am also slightly drunk is a mere irrelevance!! Can see Tate looking at badge, and try to explain about nickname and deceit of snotty-nosed wimp, but find am distracted by sight of Tate's sexy eyes and even more sexy mouth.

Wonder privately what it would be like to snog same, and then realise my wondering is not so private after all as Tate is suggesting there's only one way to find out.

Try to do decent thing and refuse to take advantage of kind-hearted American's generosity, but next thing I realise I am kneeling on Tate's chest and have pinned him to sofa whilst trying to kiss him.

I apologise immediately, but don't think Tate could have heard, 'cos suddenly I'm the one lying on sofa, with Tate on top, his hands cupping my face whilst he looks deep into my eyes and demonstrates expertise as truly awesome kisser.

Must be my lucky day!! Have propositioned Tate with an offer to show him new bra and Botox scars, and am now lying in Tate's bed having torn off clothes—Tate's, not mine!!

Mmm…he has wonderful sexy hairy chest—even better than Russell Crowe's—and I wish now that I had pinched initial badge off snotty-nosed wimp as Tate definitely outclasses footballer stud in that department!

I feel I am being invited to gorge myself on wonderful sexual banquet, and suddenly realise that marriage was sexually a semi-starvation diet!!

Later still—am totally mortified. Just as I was about to demonstrate my skills as irresistible passion-inducing partner I passed out, and now

Tate is standing next to bed—fully dressed—offering me a glass of water!!

For sake of my own pride, and to protect the innocent in the form of my future grandchildren, I am drawing a necessary veil over the rest of evening—including my return home in Tate's car and daughter's tight-lipped reception of her intoxicated semi-dressed mother!!

My mother, however, is refusing to speak to me as she is claiming I have tried to pinch her love object. I defend my actions by referring to my computer list, pointing out my dedicated desire for Tate long before mother had met him. Whilst I am talking to mother have hazy recollection of having told Tate that I'm totally in lust and in love with him, but am sure that as mature adult woman I would never have done any such thing!

Daughter is also refusing to make verbal contact with me as she claims she's totally ashamed of me after the state I was in when I was returned home last night by caring Tate.

She demands to know how I could have lowered myself to get in such a state and announces that she is thinking of booking me into a rigorous local detox centre otherwise known as Alcatraz.

I try to defend myself by explaining about lifecoach and list from *Cosmo*, but daughter has stormed out.

Go to bed to escape from raging viragos (mother and daughter), nobly refusing to give in to temptation to point out that ungrateful pair are currently living beneath my roof!!

Woken up later by raging headache and sound of doorbell ringing. I stagger downstairs in tatty old robe to discover visitor is Tate and that mother is slipping folded piece of paper into his pocket. See that mother is also flaunting plastic-reinforced body in bumster jeans and cropped top through which I can quite clearly see nipples.

She is also wearing 'shagging shoes' belonging to Cheree which she has obviously purloined from my wardrobe.

I tell mother with teeth-baring snarl that we must not delay Tate as he's no doubt on his way to see goddaughter.

Nearly faint with shock when Tate announces that goddaughter has gone home to her parents to prepare for her imminent wedding to Italian prince she met whilst skiing!!

So gossipers were wrong—stunning blonde is really goddaughter after all!!

Whilst I am glaring pointedly at mother's foot-gear, I hear Tate explaining that he has come to see if am recovered.

I thank him politely for his consideration and assure him that the whole regrettable incident was no doubt caused by stress and exhaustion due to demands of selfish and thoughtless parasites taking up houseroom that could be let to lodgers and thus earning me money.

Unfortunately daughter walks in, overhears, and announces that I am lying and I was just disgustingly drunk!

As I hurriedly show Tate to front door I feel my whole body go bright red as he leans down and whispers sexily in my ear that if I really want to remember what I said he has a very clear memory of every detail. As I am trying womanfully to look nonchalant and sophisticated, he adds in even huskier whisper that if I still want him to rip knickers off and make mad passionate love to me, then he is quite happy to oblige!!

Also says to tell mother 'thank you'!

No way am I going to share lover with own mother!! Not that Tate is own lover as yet, of course, but…

I hear a loud scream and go into kitchen to find daughter wrapping arm solicitously around nosy neighbour whilst glaring at grandmother.

Demand to know what is going on as nosy neighbour is choking and gagging and gasping that she is victim of dreadful conspiracy to poison her set up by her husband.

Mother is laughing too hard to say anything, but eventually explains that nosy neighbour has drunk contents of unmarked bottle in fridge belonging to mother.

Have to sit down as I guess it's 'the urine'.

Know it's childish, but I laugh almost as hard as mother!

CHAPTER ELEVEN

IT'S official!!! Am now another divorce statistic. Certificate arrived in post this morning—coincidentally it's also wedding anniversary, or would have been.

Telephone rings. It's son. He explains that he is not going to go back to university as he is converting to ancient religion and becoming a monk. Warmly congratulate him on his sensible career choice, which needs no financial support from me, and have to hold on to doorframe when son corrects misunderstanding and explains that he has promised ten per cent of my income to religion since he knows I would want to share in the joy of his enlightenment.

Tell him that he is to come home at once otherwise I will tell bank to foreclose on his loans!

Have decided to celebrate newly divorced status with small get-together for close friends. Jacki suggested we all go to country club bar, but when she rings to make booking she's told that we are barred.

Daughter is frostily disapproving of whole idea of celebration. I suggest sarcastically that I suppose I should be wearing sackcloth and ashes, whereupon daughter promptly bursts into tears and demands to know if I realise that I have robbed her of her father.

Point out that it was hardly much loss, since father more of a liability than an asset.

When daughter remains po-faced, I remind her of how she used to beg me not to let father attend any school functions in case anyone realised they were related.

Daughter denies any such request.

Am just preparing simple little buffet for friends—e.g. hardening soft old crackers in oven whilst sending mother out into garden to find some greenery to decorate plates artistically!

In two minds whether or not to invite Tate—can still remember how Jacki stole first boyfriend—and second and third. But then it would be a good way to show him that I am accomplished house-wife and minor domestic goddess—after all, well known that the way to a man's heart is through his stomach!!

However, train of thought interrupted when discover that dog has licked all pâté off carefully prepared feast, so have to ring round friends and explain that I forgot to mention on original invite that party is 'bring a plate' event!!

Am just testing wine with Daniel when phone rings. Am astonished to discover caller is ex-husband—wonder if has forgotten we are now di-

vorced and is ringing to wish me happy anniversary?

However, realise that ex has just read out-of-
date copy of newspaper article about desirability
and rocketing prices of property in our road. Ex
practically frothing at mouth with excitement and
announces that he is on way home to supervise sale
and that I am on no account to accept any offer
under £l0m.

Point out very gently to ex that house is now
totally in my name and remind him that this was
his idea. Also remind him equally gently that we
are now divorced and then tell him that if he tele-
phones again will report him to police for harassment.

As I replace receiver I hear combined sound of
anguished whisper and unnervingly demented
scream.

Must remember to congratulate and thank golf
club president's ex-wife for little tips on how to
make divorce more pleasant and exact revenge on
greedy selfish husband. Must say it was v. clever
of her to suggest contacting friend who's a newspaper journalist who owed her a favour. In return
have given her transcript of golf club president's
telephone call with me on sex chat line!!
Understand she has plans to have it broadcast all
over golf course during most important match of
the season!!

*   *   *

Am too overwhelmed to know how to write about party!!

Guests arrived on time, with 'plates', and announced they were mystified as to why I wanted them as they knew I had my own excellent dinner service.

I was too busy pouring drinks at first to realise that 'plates' were all friends had brought.

Asked red-faced with temper if all friends were completely stupid and said I had meant *food*. I could see one or two looking huffy, but scene was averted when ring of doorbell heralded arrival of yummy pizza deliveries ordered by kind, thoughtful, wonderful friends who pretended to misunderstand initial request as joke!!

Ha-ha… Am really in party mood now!!! Hate pizza—especially when delivered cold by spotty youth who is picking nose.

Doorbell rings again, so open it and yell that can he stuff pizza where sun doesn't shine—only isn't pizza delivery man but Tate!!

Why does this always happen to me?

Totter off to kitchen and find dog sulking in front of Aga. Realise it is night for her favourite programme, so switch on kitchen TV. Soon am sobbing my heart out over plight of unwanted puppies found at side of road. Have to switch off programme as is too upsetting.

Hear my name being called by guests high on carbohydrate and E numbers. Go into sitting room and discover I have forgotten to switch off special sex line phone. Guests are demanding to know if caller is up to satisfying thirty raunchy women, and also if his mother knows what he is doing!

Caller slams down phone, which rings again within minutes. It is call centre manager saying that I am fired.

I go upstairs to bathroom and find mother in bedroom with Tate. Throw immediate tantrum and lock myself in bathroom, refusing to come out. Fortunately have stashed secret supply of Georgette Heyer novels in airing cupboard.

Eventually come out in early hours of morning. All guests have gone. Can't decide who I hate most—mother or Tate!!

CHAPTER TWELVE

I AM now totally reformed. Well, I had to after daughter and nosy neighbour had to prise my hands from round mother's neck when I attacked her in fit of jealous fury over her deliberate (unsuccessful) attempt to seduce Tate.

Mother claims she's made a total error of judgement and is planning to return to States as it's only place she can have scratches on her neck properly fixed.

Have also had row with nosy neighbour over her plan to erect huge telescope in garden—am sure she is lying about interest in astronomy, especially since I found book on blackmail in her wardrobe.

Am frantic with worry. Dog is missing! Daughter left back gate open. Claims it was a mistake, but I know she does not like dog. Am bereft. Dog has become closer to me than my children. Am beside myself with anxiety. Have rung police station and pet shop, but both have refused to give me name of couple who own Floor Mop and I dare not ask silver wedding party neighbour.

Mother now claims she has communicated with dog and has discovered time of birth from which she has plotted natal chart. She says that dog has Scorpio rising, which explains high sex drive. No doubt mother has same, as she has everything rising.

In midst of this I hear scrabbling at door. Hurry to open and discover dog standing there. She has something in her mouth.

Feel faint with dread as I contemplate the possibility that Sheba has raped and abducted Floor Mop, but dog is now lying beside Aga and I realise when she releases bundle of fur from her mouth that it is not Floor Mop but in fact a puppy dog.

Once I am over shock, I demand that mother communicates with dog and finds out what is happening.

Mother gets on high horse and refuses!! Try to pick up puppy, with intention of taking same to dog pound, but dog bares teeth and gives me a look of warning.

Television is on and suddenly hear announcement on local news about theft of very valuable pedigree puppies. Police apparently taking matter very seriously and criminal will be prosecuted and sent to prison.

Go to ring police and explain about own innocence and non-involvement, but now have no local police station and call is re-routed to call centre fifty miles away where they know nothing about stolen puppies and demand that I stop wasting valuable police time.

Get back to kitchen to discover that dog has gone again. Pick up puppy, who promptly growls, nips finger and wees on skirt.

I demand that mother proves her whispering skill by communicating with puppy, but she is still in a strop and refuses.

Whilst in middle of argument with mother dog returns—and has another puppy in her mouth. Whilst I am worrying about what to do doorbell rings. Try to hide, in case it's police with a warrant, but mother answers and comes back with Tate.

I reluctantly explain what has happened and then realise that dog is making for still open door. I go to close it, but Tate shakes head and whispers that I should let her go and follow so that we can discover where she is getting the puppies from.

It is good idea, but I point out snappily to mother that there is no need to behave as though he has just invented rocket science.

Mother has suggested that I follow dog on foot whilst she and Tate trail in car.

Why do I always fall for it? Am now breathless and scratched from close encounters with dangerous forms of wildlife in shape of children on bikes and skateboards, not to mention a crazy driver who attempted to pin me to a wall when I tried to cross at traffic lights.

Dog is making for the allotments and railway embankment. Remember now that she had to be called back when on a walk the previous day as she was sniffing round shed. I thought it might be because it's known to be used by courting couples.

Am so out of breath that I have to stop, but fortunately mother has co-opted Tate's new four-wheel drive.

I finally catch up with dog outside tatty garden shed on neglected and overgrown allotment.

Dog barks, and then wriggles under shed, returning with pup.

I get down on my hands and knees and with help of Tate and mother discover two more pups in under-shed den.

We return to house in four-wheel drive with pups.

The dog and pups gather cosily round Aga. Mother triumphantly announces that she has been informed by dog that dog learned of pups' presence whilst on a walk and thought instantly of abandoned babies she had seen on TV programme. Naturally her maternal urges were aroused—apparently vet has not disclosed to me that due to dog's attack on assistant, her operation was never actually completed!! Dog has made dignified and sorrowful admission that she is currently suffering from empty basket syndrome, hence reckless attempted seduction of only male dog she has seen.

Dog has apparently already decided that pups are best with her until she is sure that suitable homes will be found. Pups are too young to remember own mother, but do remember that they were fed top-quality dog food.

Am taken out of kitchen by Tate, who informs me that he suspects pups are actually the stolen litter and that own dog is a heroine for having found them.

Thankfully agree that Tate should be one to inform police of dog's noble bravery and resourcefulness!!

Three hours later—pups have finally been reunited with owner and mother dog. A most emotional and touching scene when large hairy woman arrived with equally large hairy dog to inspect pups and confirm that they are missing litter.

A pity that Sheba was so aggressive with mother dog, but finally managed to persuade her to relinquish final pup by mother's whispered intervention.

Local reporter has called round to do in-depth interview with canine mother and—via my mother—Sheba, and also local Animal Rescue Centre, which is to nominate Sheba for Dog of Year award.

They have now all gone and I am cooing over wonderful clever dog and promising that I will definitely replace disgusting cheap food with genuine superior dog food.

Am just about to sneak off for reviving read of Georgette Heyer, and to fantasise about Tate, when I remember to ask mother what she whispered to dog to get her to drop last puppy.

Mother gives me an innocent look that makes my heart sink and claims that she said nothing, really—only that if Sheba gave up the pup, she would insist that I made arrangements for Sheba to have intimate candlelit bowl of top quality dog food with top stud dog of the same breed so that she could have pups of her own...

Next day come downstairs to discover that dog is a national heroine, with her picture in all national dailies. Phone is ringing non-stop with people requesting interviews with dog and dog-whispering mother.

Am just listening with great delight to one reporter describing mother as sweet, gentle, innocent old lady when said sweet, gentle, innocent old lady bursts into kitchen and announces that she believes Daniel and daughter have reached mutual understanding and settled differences.

I deny that they can have done any such thing. Mother responds that it's either that or they have been attempting to murder one another, judging from intensity of headboard-banging against adjoining wall last night—three times and twice this morning!

Am lost for words, but then suddenly remember gorgeous baby outfit I saw in a local shop window and wonder if they still have it.

Daniel arrives in kitchen and announces tersely that he is moving out.

Daughter arrives in kitchen and announces she is moving out.

Ask sarcastically if mutual move anything to do with banging taking place in bedroom.

Daughter promptly bursts into tears. Daniel takes her protectively in arms and dries tears with edge of own tee shirt.

Daughter hiccups that she cannot commit to a relationship based only on sex.

Daniel asks why not, and says anyway it's not just based on sex as they have other things in common—or hopefully they will soon, he adds meaningfully.

Am now really determined to see if baby outfit still there, and am v. disappointed when daughter shrieks that she does not want either his body or his job.

After Daniel has left room, I tell daughter she is complete fool for preferring weak commitment-phobe Brian when she could have sexy and hunky commitment-minded Daniel.

Daughter says scornfully that no one is that much of a fool—and anyway who is Brian? She is just nobly renouncing Daniel out of deep love for him as she does not want to trap him in sex-based marriage.

Tell daughter she is off rocker and should take Daniel out for celebratory meal and purchase a huge diamond ring immediately.

CHAPTER THIRTEEN

AM COMPLETELY alone in the house as mother has gone out and Daniel and daughter have gone to look at a new private little nest they can share now that they are officially engaged.

Nosy neighbour has become v. friendly with large hairy woman who owns dog and has been invited to move in with her.

Am just contemplating own lonely and sad future when doorbell rings.

Go to answer it and discover Tate standing on doorstep. As he comes in he says in v. businesslike manner that he has come about the list.

I am confused, and assume he must be collecting names for something. Ask if it's anything to do with the condoms nosy neighbour used to collect from the local park, as I know she had intended to send the council angry list of complaints about it.

Tate answers 'Not exactly,' and then walks into kitchen and pulls down blind. Also ejects dog.

He still has paper in hand and is frowning as he studies it. Am further confused when he starts to remove jacket and begins to unfasten shirt.

Realise he has put the list down, and see to my horror that it is my own list of life goals, including secret wish list of raunchy sex with Tate…

Whilst I am recovering breath and easing cramp out of my knees, Tate lowers me from kitchen table to floor and asks solicitously if there are any other positions I want to try incorporating kitchen equipment.

Am too exhausted to speak, so have to shake head.

Tate announces that he is glad because now we have got that out of way he is going to take me upstairs and make love to me until I give in and agree that I will become his wife.

Am dreaming… Must be… Mmm… Mmmm… Tate is a very good snogger…

Is no good—have had to give in! Am to marry Tate as soon as it can be arranged!! Discover that he fell in love with me at first sight, but had thought I was involved with Daniel!

Fondly say he is a total fool, and then admit that I believed he had lied about goddaughter and she was really his live-in lover.

Both agree it was a silly mistake, then Tate confides that he only realised truth about my feelings when mother gave him the computer list.

Mother is not a witch—she's a good fairy!!!

We are just trying out interesting improvisation on missionary position when remember dog is still outside and it's long past mealtime—decide improvisation too interesting to ignore—unlike howls of dog…

EPILOGUE

CAN'T believe Tate and me have been married for a whole year, or that I am grandmother to adorable pair of twins. Mother has refused to acknowledge true relationship to twins and is telling everyone that she's their aunt!!

Tate and I are now living in wonderful country house which I am in process of redecorating. Tate says doesn't care what I do so long as I don't plan to take in lodgers.

I would never do that—privacy is an essential ingredient to our v. special sex life—after all, how could we make love naked in the garden as dawn is breaking if I had lodgers? Or in front of the fire on cold nights on a sheepskin rug... Or, best of all, in our wonderful huge bed in our own bedroom. It is wonderful being married to sexiest man on earth!!! And he can make me laugh too!!!

Even so, I do enjoy visits from family and am looking forward to busy Christmas—with Daniel and daughter, plus twins, and Georgie and Erica, plus son and soon-to-be-born second baby, along with my mother and her new husband, who I haven't met as yet but who she promises I will like. Of course will have to invite nosy neighbour and 'friend'—i.e. hairy dog-owner—otherwise Sheba will go into terminal sulk. Discovered that hairy woman had prize-winning super-stud male German Shepherd and as reward for Sheba's cleverness agreed that they could mate.

Three pups were born—have kept one ourselves, Daniel and daughter have one and Georgie and Erica have the other!

Only slight cloud on horizon is threatened return of son now that he has finished university course (he gave up life as a monk eventually because of lack of funds and went back to college). But Tate has cleverly suggested he can get him a job in his company—in the Washington, USA, branch! Not that I don't love my son—I do. But I'm still too much in love with Tate to want anyone else in the house.

Oh, almost forgot. Tate has confided that he adores my boobs and does not think they're droopy at all but wonderfully sexy, squidgy and real. Says adult male human beings are not designed to enjoy raw and immature fruit, and many other flattering things that I'm not going to repeat here!!

Am happiest woman in whole world!!!

A GIRL'S
BEST FRIEND

by
DARCY MAGUIRE

Darcy Maguire wanted to grow up to be a fairy, but her wings never grew, her magic never worked and her life was no fairytale. But one thing she knew for certain was that she was going to find her soul-mate and live happily ever after. Darcy found her dark and handsome hero on a blind date, married him a year later and found that love truly is the soul of creativity.

With four children too young to play matchmaker for (yet!), Darcy satisfies the romantic in her by finding true love for her fictional characters. It was this passion for romance, and her ability to sit still every day, that led to the publication of her first novel, HER MARRIAGE SECRET. Darcy lives in Melbourne, Australia, and loves to read widely, sew and sneak off to the movies without the kids.

Look out for future novels by Darcy Maguire in Tender Romance™.

CHAPTER ONE

I PICKED George up on a street corner on a rainy day. His deep dark eyes drew me under his spell and his soft voice tugged at my heart that was hidden deeply that day beneath layer upon layer of coat and woollies to protect me from Melbourne's bitter winter winds. I'd fallen in love at first sight. I only wish he'd been a man, and not a dog.

I ran a hand through George's coat. He was having a really bad hair month, being a Maltese terrier crossed with a bit of this and a bit of everything else in the gene pool—there must have been a few bitches in the bloodline with great big smiles on their faces!

As I watched the movie I snuggled closer to George's warm body, half tempted to pull my quilt over the top of us to save on the heating bill, but loath even to move. I was riveted to the spot.

She was going to fall into his trap. He was a man, and all men were liars. I knew it. Everyone knew it. Why didn't she wake up to the fact and save herself the pain?

I bit the end of my fingernail and watched helplessly as she looked at him with her innocent, loving eyes.

159

The tall, dark, delicious guy dropped to one knee and gazed up into her eager face. 'You're the most wonderful person in the world. I want to share my life with you. Please, will you marry me?'

I smothered my face in the pillow. I knew what was coming. I'd seen him with that other woman and I knew what he was. Why couldn't she see it? Why was she being such a fool?

'Yes, of course I will,' she whispered. And they kissed.

My eyes were glued to the screen. It looked like love and it sounded like love, and that kiss had looked absolutely divine. I touched my lips softly. How long had it been since I was kissed? I shook my head. I didn't want to think about it.

The scene faded out and commercials bombarded the screen.

I rolled over on my bed and stared at the ceiling. How could she be such a fool? He was going to betray her, just as he'd betrayed his ex-wife. It was obvious. So obvious I could live without dragging myself through the emotional quagmire that was going to follow.

I grabbed the remote, aimed, and snapped the telly off. I didn't need to watch any more. I knew exactly what was going to happen. There wasn't going to be a happy ending, and as far as I'm concerned a story without a happy ending isn't worth the effort.

So much for watching a good movie to distract me.

There was nothing else for it.

I rolled off my patchwork bedspread, pushing off a dozen chocolate bar wrappers as I went, and snatched up the peach satin dress I'd flung over a chair almost a fortnight ago.

I held it up against my body, stifling the urge to cry again. How could I watch my best friend, my last single friend, get married?

I dropped my dressing gown to the floor, slipped off my pyjamas and slid my arms into the smooth, cool fabric. If I was going to have to wear it tomorrow, I wanted to know what sort of bimbo I was going to look like.

I stared at my reflection and pulled a face. I ran my hands over my hips, shaking my head. How was I going to fit into the bridesmaid's dress with last week's chocolate binge sitting thick and heavy on my curves?

I slipped into the outfit.

The peach satin fabric clung to my curves faithfully down to my knees—though I couldn't remember it being this tight at the last fitting—in a modern, as opposed to Cinderella sort of way. The get-up made the most of my cleavage, which had grown with the rest of me.

Thank goodness there was some good to come out of all that chocolate!

I cringed at my reflection. I didn't know why I'd let the hairdresser convince me a bob was the perfect cut for me. So it might be easy to maintain, and it might make the most of the shape of my face, but it had the terrible side effect of making me look sweet! And I didn't want to look sweet— 'sweet' just wasn't in!

I gathered up my short brown hair and pinned it roughly at my nape. I turned around in front of the mirror—better. Almost elegant.

I offered myself a soft smile in the mirror. I could almost imagine the dress being white. Just add a veil and I'd be the bride… Oh, and add a groom of some description—no point in being a bride without having a groom.

I waltzed out of my bedroom and plucked a flower from the vase on the table, clutching it to my ribs as though it were a bouquet. I floated through my apartment, casting my eyes to one side, then the other, smiling at my haphazard bits of furniture as though they were my friends and family watching me float down the aisle.

My round dining table was my cousin, with her brood of four. My soft blue lounge suite was my uncle and aunt. The coffee table was a deep mahogany, like my parents' retriever cross—though what the dog was doing at my wedding, I didn't know. The hall table was my cousin Colin, tall and spindly, with the weight of the world on his shoulders—or, in this case, the entire contents of my three handbags and last month's mail.

I reached the front door, which would've done for a priest. But there was no groom. Wasn't likely to be. But what did I expect…?

I'm a born-again virgin. You know, the sort of woman who takes herself out of playing the field in an effort to find herself. I hadn't found me. All I'd found was that time had passed me by and I was looking at another birthday. And not just any birthday—my twenty-sixth.

A lot of us women use numbers as motivation: how much your ideal weight should be, how many men to date before you settle, how many slices of pizza is too many, how many drinks you need before the reality of your life fades… For me, I have a use-by date.

I've been counting down since I was nine. It was the day after my birthday and David Middleborough had just jilted me. My belly still rolled at the memory. All it had taken was for my best friend—make that ex-best friend—to wave a double choc ice cream under his nose and he was gone.

I had decided on the spot I was going to get married as soon as I could, so I didn't have to put myself out there and face the sort of rejection I'd had that day. I was going to get my own boy, tie him to me with the bonds of marriage, and I was going to live happily ever after. And if I hadn't by the time I was twenty-six I was going to become a nun.

I'd waved my share of chocolate ice creams in front of boys since then. Actually, I'd waved all sorts of things in front of boys. And I'd got them. But I learned pretty damn quickly that there's a certain type of boy you want to keep, and a certain type you want to avoid at all costs. But, hell, even after years of practice I couldn't work out which was which until it was too late. So I quit trying. I pulled myself off the field, off the shelf, out of the dating game.

The nun thing is no longer a part of the equation, but there is still that deep desire to marry a man, which until now I had pushed to the back of my mind. It's certainly been better for my sanity to concentrate wholly and entirely on my career.

I strode back to my room, the dress peach again, my veil gone, my imagination AWOL. I dropped onto my bed and George leapt up beside me, snuggling under my arm, licking my hand and panting in my face.

I rubbed his back—where would I be without him? He was my rock. I looked into his deep brown eyes and buried my face in his neck. He always knew when I was down and needed a cuddle, unlike any other male in my life!

I guess I wouldn't have minded so much about turning a very single twenty-six if all my friends hadn't got married. Caitlin was the last one—my last single friend, my flatmate, my confidante. What was I going to do? Find new friends or get married? Was George my new best friend?

I sat up and smoothed down the dress, determined to pull myself together. I was a very capable, mature, independent woman. I was going to get on with *my life*.

I stared out of the window, right into Courtney Jenkins' apartment next door. In reality, the brand-spanking-new building was barely fifteen metres away from my own, space being at a premium this close to Melbourne's central business district, and views being sacrificed to make way for the yuppies. But it felt closer. And it beat television most nights.

Watching someone else's life unfold made me feel a part of something. Until she closed the curtains anyway. And, no, I'm not some peeping pervert. Courtney across the way and I are friends. Okay, so she isn't a close friend. So, we hardly speak at all. But she's single—with a little boy. We do say hello, and pass the time with each other on the street, and wave when we catch each other looking.

I sometimes wonder if she ever thinks about what it would be like to be in my shoes, because I certainly think about what it would be like to be in hers. Having a little boy to look after, to call your own, to share your life with, to live your life for, to give you a reason to leap out of bed each day…

The knock on the door startled me. I wasn't expecting anyone, but anybody would be better company than I was being to myself in this mood. I almost ran to the door.

Al Blight stood there, filling my front doorway as if he owned it—which he did. Or as good as. He ran the apartment block as though he was Commander in Chief of everybody and everything.

He wasn't a small man. He was as wide as he was tall, with long black hair, greased back against his skull, and beady black eyes set deep in his face.

'Morning, Casey.' He stroked his grey-spattered beard with one hand. The other was shoved deeply in his trouser pocket as he stared at my B-cup-going-on-C-cup breasts. 'You know how you like to collect strays…?'

I kept my face impassive. I didn't intend to look concerned that he knew about more than just George. It was enough he knew about one illegal pet. I could see the mad glint of power in his eyes already, and I knew, right down to my little toe, that I was in for it.

He'd caught me sneaking out for a walk last week with my little ball of sunshine under my coat. I hadn't had a minute's peace since, worrying over what he was going to do about it. Now, it seemed, I was going to find out.

'I have one more for you.' Al laughed, though it sounded more like a phlegmy wheeze. 'My cousin needs a place for a few weeks—maybe a month. And I know Caitlin's getting married, so you must need another roomie to make the rent.'

Al shot me a look, knowing full well that Caitlin had moved out a fortnight ago. 'I know your job doesn't pay enough. The rent here is quite beyond the average secretary—unless you've been upped to PA?'

I sucked in a deep breath, reminding myself to be civil. I hadn't told him I'd finally left my secretarial job and started work as a veterinary assistant at the end of last year. The night school had paid off. *I was finally doing a job I loved.*

'Thank you for your concern, but I'm fine,' I said, pouring on my silky-smooth office voice that I usually reserved just for the boss—or, nowadays, for a distressed pet-owner—to lull him into my way of thinking. But by the look on Al's face he was immune. And he knew as well as I did that he had me right where he wanted me—in trouble.

I straightened, mounting my case in my mind. I had some money saved—okay, a tiny cache of spare change. But it wasn't enough to pay for this place on my own.

Of course, I'd planned to stop shopping and start saving soon, but I wasn't through sulking over Caitlin abandoning me for some cute suit. And I wasn't going to accept some relative of Al's in her place—she'd snitch on me about everything. 'Why don't you offer one of *your* rooms?'

He shifted on his large, flat feet. 'We're not that close. Did I mention I'm making out the monthly report right now? I'd hate for me to have to request a certain eviction notice be sent out for breach of terms.' He stroked his beard meaningfully. 'Like the one about no pets.'

My body chilled. I couldn't lose George—as well as Caitlin—or be out on the streets. Good places in the inner city are hard to find. 'Okay, fine. If your cousin comes up with some references that I can check there's no problem.' I said it quickly—I didn't want him to be suspicious.

There was no way I wanted him to start thinking seriously about what else I'd sneaked past him and had living in my apartment. I shot him a pleasant smile. I'd deal with his cousin, whatever challenge she brought.

I closed the door and leant against it, my mind a mass of tangled thoughts. What was I going to do with the rest of my babies? I couldn't see them go—they were like family. I nibbled on my lower lip. How could I get out of sharing my sanctuary with a relative of the enemy? Could I scare her off?

My life couldn't get any worse.

The knock on my door thudded right through me. I jumped. I didn't need another visitor just now. I was tempted to ignore it and crawl back to bed, and try to forget about the whole weekend.

The knocks got louder.

I turned and opened the door, fully expecting to see Al standing there, adding something else to the 'favour', or just drumming up another opportunity to peer at my breasts.

It wasn't Al.

The cutest guy I'd seen in the flesh since the stripping hunks at Caitlin's hen night stood on my. doorstep His long legs were clad in blue denim jeans and I tilted my head to see if his butt was as good as the guy in the jeans ad—and from this angle, I would have to say it was better. A plain black T-shirt hugged his well-built chest, but he could have been naked for all the rippling detail it afforded. He had a tan leather jacket casually slung over one of his solid shoulders, and was looking cool, casual and confident. His dark hair was short, his jaw strong and clean-shaven, and his eyes…

'Yes?' I managed finally, my voice thin and tight. What did this guy want on my doorstep? He could have been a strippergram for the woman down the hall...

'You're expecting me?' His voice was deep and warm and as good as the rest of him.

'No.'

'Didn't Alan speak to you?' His brow furrowed and his seriously handsome smile transformed into a frown.

My heart leapt to my throat. Oh, God. No. He couldn't be. I ran my eyes slowly up the man's body, up the long legs, over the flat waist, over the muscled torso. Up over his sensuous lips and into his deep, dark eyes. I swallowed. 'You're not his cousin?'

'Yes, I am,' he said easily.

Never in my life could I have imagined Al's cousin to look like this. This was the sort of guy my nightmares were made of. Okay, my dreams too. But, hell, every guy that had tramped over my heart had come in a package no different from this guy's—tall, dark and devilishly handsome. The bane of my life!

How was I going to deal with *him* in my apartment? In my life? I wasn't ready to put my new-found skills into practice. I needed more than skills to keep me safe from this guy. It was time to become a nun!

CHAPTER TWO

'HERE are my references.' He shoved a wad of papers towards me. One of his large square hands held the sheets on one side, his long thumb keeping them together, stretched almost halfway across the papers.

My mind darted to how long his fingers must be, hiding on the other side, how strong and gentle and persuasive they'd be all over my body...

My blood heated. My cheeks warmed—as did other places I'd rather have forgotten about. I swallowed, stifling the irritating response. 'That was quick.'

'I'm a fast worker.'

I stared at him. I could imagine him being a fast worker on more fronts than just his references. And I could tell just by the way he stood there on my doorstep, oozing a commanding presence, that he wasn't used to coming off second best in anything. I straightened to my full height, tilting my chin up and looking the guy directly in the chin.

I took the proffered papers, careful not to touch him. Hell, I was having trouble thinking straight just looking at him, let alone touching any part of his too-good-to-be-true body.

I stared at the pages, but couldn't get my eyes to focus on the damned things. I couldn't imagine what he was thinking of me wearing the damned peach dress on a Saturday morning! I jerked my mind back to reality and logic. What did I care what he thought?

He took my attire in his stride—I figured he'd take everything that came his way in his stride. 'Are you going to invite me in?' he asked, raising an eyebrow.

I'd have rather swum with piranhas. I knew exactly what this guy was all about and I wanted nothing whatsoever to do with him. 'No.'

He crossed his arms over his chest, which had somehow grown even larger, straining against the fabric of his shirt. He gave me a stern look. 'I understand you and Alan have an arrangement?'

I stepped back. 'An arrangement?' That sounded far too intimate for me. 'I'd rather describe it as a blackmail.'

'I had an inkling.'

His casual tone seared me. He didn't care! It was sickeningly obvious there was no point in doing the damsel-in-distress act with this guy. I crossed my arms over my chest, sucking in air, hoping it would grow in proportion, as his had. 'And what sort of inkling would that be?'

He nodded to George, who was busy polishing the front entry with his tail. The corners of the guy's mouth threatened to erupt into a smile, as though he thought it was funny I could be black-mailed over a dog.

I bit my lip, stifling the swell of anger. He knew everything. Damn. That gave him more clout than I wanted him to have.

George came up beside me. He nudged my leg with his head and looked up at me. I felt the pit of my stomach turn into ice. I knew I couldn't refuse this guy. I needed George. And Al had a good point about the money. I could do with let-ting out the room. But to this guy? Never! Every part of my body screamed no. But did I have a choice?

I would have to be tough...and I wouldn't have to put up with him for long. Even if I couldn't hurry him along, what could a couple of weeks hurt? I wasn't the same guy-crazed female I'd been last year. I was in control—totally in control of myself. And nothing was going to get the better of me, or my new-found judgement, especially not a guy like this.

I let him in.

It was crazy.

I'd been to enough self-defence classes to think this was not a good idea. And I'd been celibate long enough to know this was *definitely* not a good idea.

My hands itched as he moved past me, and I sucked in a long, deep breath to steady myself. There was no way I was going to start chanting affirmations. I didn't need to. I was a strong, independent woman who had a firm control on her mind and body. I threw back my shoulders and closed the door behind him, trying to keep my eyes off his really cute butt as he sauntered into my lounge room in those sexy-as-hell tight denims.

I let out my breath in a rush and followed him into the lounge. 'Please, sit down and we'll discuss this,' I said, as calmly as a flight attendant, though I was feeling everything but calm!

I rubbed my hands on my dress. Okay, I was losing all my 'tough' pretty damned quick. So there was nothing else for it—I had to give him a good reason to go somewhere else. Easy.

I watched the guy sling his jacket over the arm-rest of the sofa and sit down, his legs wide, his elbows on his knees, staring intently at…me.

My stomach tingled annoyingly and my blood warmed, all the way to my cheeks. 'I can't possibly share my apartment with you,' I blurted.

He raised one eyebrow. 'Firstly, I understand how you feel.'

Sure he did.

George nudged his knee. He bent down and gave my dog a thorough rub behind his ears, working his way down his neck, giving him a thorough work-over. 'You don't know me. So let me remedy that.'

I held my breath. My mind darted to all the ways we could get better acquainted, and none of them included words…

I stifled the thought—what was he doing to me?

'My name is Richard Hunter. I'm from Brisbane.' He patted George's butt and he sat down at his feet, staring up at this new guy with puppy eyes. 'You can call me Rick.'

'Stop.' I didn't want to call him anything. I didn't want to know anything about him. The more he'd tell me the more I'd feel obligated to let him stay. 'I don't want to know you. I will not share my apartment with you.'

'I'm quiet, a non-smoker, clean—' He shot an assessing glance around my lounge area, and then gave me a dubious look.

So, there were a few magazines scattered around—a year's worth. So, there were a few clothes too—probably enough to make a load in the washer. So, there were a few dishes tucked here and there—plenty more still in the cupboard.

'And I can pay in advance,' he stated, with a certainty that this fact should end all my qualms.

I stared at him. He was saying all the right things. Suspiciously so. I narrowed my eyes. I wasn't born yesterday.

I shook my head.

'Because I'm a man?'

Because he was the most sexy man I'd been near in ages! Certainly he was the most sexy man I'd spoken to for aeons—unless you counted screaming 'Get it off!' to the stripper at the hen night.

I counted to ten. Slowly. I wasn't going to agree with him—there was no way I was going to openly admit I was scared to death.

Of him? Or was it of myself falling into his arms? I clenched my hands in front of me, standing frozen to the spot, not about to step one inch closer to the guy.

He stood up, pacing the floor as though he couldn't sit idle any longer. 'I can guarantee you that there won't be any problems on that front.'

He could guarantee he wasn't going to jump me? I felt a little miffed. How could he be certain? Wasn't I his type? What *was* his type? I was tall, dark and able...was he into blondes?

'Why's that?' The words fell from my mouth.

'I'm...' He averted his eyes and stared towards the window. 'I'm...married.'

The air in my lungs stuck. Married. My mind froze. Married? My knees gave out beneath me and I sagged, right into the nearest chair. Married!

He didn't look married. He radiated a very available charm. His body screamed very available S-E-X. And his lips—his lips begged to be kissed. My eyes darted to his left hand. He covered it.

'I…I don't wear a ring.'

Why? So he could torture all women every-where with fantasies of what it would be like to have him touch, kiss, take…?

'Really? And she can do without you for a while?'

He strode to the window, staring at Courtney Jenkins' flat across the way. He finally turned.

'I'm…writing a…book.' He paused. 'I needed…some space.' A longer silence. 'She's fine with it. I thought old Alan would set me up with a room, no worries.' He glanced back across the way. 'But…Alan being Alan, he's left me stranded. I apologise for any inconvenience but I really, truly need some quiet time to myself to get this…book…going in the right direction.'

I almost closed my eyes, to let his deep velvet voice wash over me, but I couldn't miss looking at him. I knew I was being stupid, ogling him like a schoolgirl, but goodness, I was human…and way too female to ignore his attributes.

There was no chance I could let him stay in my place, my haven, my sanctuary. Though there had to be some merit in him confessing he was married as opposed to pretending to be something he wasn't… And then there was George. I watched my George wagging his tail at Rick Hunter's feet. I didn't have a choice.

I sucked in a deep breath. I had to admit I felt better about it knowing he was absolutely no threat to me if he was *happily* married. He was happy? 'How long have you been married?'

He looked up at the ceiling. 'Ah…nearly…two years.'

I let my eyes wander over his lean, smoothly muscled body. 'And she'll be okay about you sharing a place with a single woman?'

He nodded, casting another look out of the window.

I should have added that this single woman figured she was okay-looking, very available and, at this present point in time, desperate for a man's touch. For the right guy's touch, of course. I jerked back to reality. Where had that come from? I was happy! And, even if he *was* available, this guy would *never* be the right guy.

'She'll probably visit, then?' I asked hopefully. I would be very interested to see what sort of woman turned Mr Fantastic here into a love-puppy. And she'd be a great reminder of where to keep my thoughts and hands—to myself.

He nodded. 'Sure.'

He didn't sound so sure. 'Everything fine with your marriage?' I had to ask. Curiosity being a bane I have to live with.

'Perfect.' He stared out of the window again, and smiled. 'Absolutely perfect.'

I could hear it in his voice. He was content. I had nothing to worry about—except keeping my libido in check with Mr Wonderful waltzing around the apartment.

I squirmed in my seat, taking deep breaths, praying for my pulse to slow and my blood to cool. I had to get rid of the guy. And fast.

The reception rooms were exquisite. Light cascaded from multi-tiered chandeliers onto marble floors; the high ceilings and pastel walls, the silver cutlery and fine china on pristine white tablecloths, all contributed to the mood—simple elegance, on a grand scale. There was enough room to play a game of rugby in the place. And, believe me, there were more than a few single women ready to tackle the bachelors in the room. But not me.

Caitlin and her hubby swept across the dance floor with the music. I smiled, feeling the warm glow inside me bounce around a bit. She made a beautiful bride. They made a wonderful couple. I crossed my fingers and said a prayer. I hope it lasts. They'd met in one of those heaven-sent love-at-first-sight meetings across a crowded shopping mall.

I would have cried at the wedding if I'd let myself, but I steadfastly refused to dwell on the fact that I was a bridesmaid again and not a bride. I had no one to blame but myself. And Alex, Tom,

Jack, Steve, Joel, Ben, Simon, Kevin, Tony, David…

'Would you like to dance?'

I turned to face a nice-looking young man beaming at me. I shook my head. Not a chance. I knew where a dance took me. I knew where a date took me. I'd been there one too many times for my liking, and I'd had enough pain and embarrassment for one lifetime.

'No, but thank you.' It was the one skill I'd gained in the last year and a half—to say no. And what a big one that was to learn…

The man walked away without looking back.

I was glad. I was still strong. Still tough. Having Rick in my apartment wasn't going to change anything. So he was seriously cute. It didn't change who I was and what I wanted.

My friend Sophie, who was married two years ago to an accountant—she met him at an office party and fell into his arms, literally—grabbed me and pulled me to her table. 'So, tell me all the goss. How's life without Caitlin? How are your pets? When are you going to find Mr Right and join us old married women?' She sucked in a deep breath. 'When are we coming to your wedding?'

'When I find the right man,' I said, without enthusiasm. 'What's all the hype about having a husband anyway?'

'It's not about having a hubby. It's about having someone to share your life with.' Sophie tossed her mane of bleached blonde hair and gave me a soft smile of encouragement.

'I've got George,' I countered.

'George is a dog.'

'Thanks, I had noticed that.' I took a gulp of champagne from my glass. Gosh, with all the help from my friends it was a wonder I was sane, let alone single.

Sophie leant closer to me, touching my arm. 'And when are you going to realise that's not enough?'

I tipped my chin high. 'When I'm good and ready.'

Sophie watched the couples on the dance floor, probably concocting a new way to trap me into saying I was lonely. 'So, what's new in your life?'

'How about six feet of prime male?' I couldn't resist teasing her. It was worth the effort. Her look of stunned amazement was priceless.

Sophie's eyes widened.

I laughed. 'He's not mine. He's well and truly spoken for. But he's nice to look at.'

'How? Why? Where?' she demanded.

'He came to the door—the landlord's cousin—and begged me to let him rent out Caitlin's room.'

Sophie leant forward, her eyes gleaming. 'And you said no?'

'Of course I did. But Al's blackmailing me into it.' I took another gulp of the bubbly and pouted. 'Mr Rick Hunter just came by to show me his references. He's writing a book, you know.'

Her eyes widened. 'How did you leave it?'

I shrugged. 'He knew I had no choice. He was just being polite.' In a really irritatingly civilised sort of way.

'So when's he moving in?'

I paused. 'No idea.' I shrugged. 'Hopefully never.'

But I knew my luck wasn't that good. I crossed my fingers under the table. I hoped to have at least a few days before he shifted his gorgeous butt into my spare room. I had to sort everything out. Self included.

The speakers shrieked. Everyone looked to the dais to see the culprit with the microphone. 'Gather around, all you single ladies. The bride is about to throw her bouquet,' the groom announced with enthusiasm.

A squeal rose up from the throng of people. Women of all shapes and sizes rushed out onto the dance floor. I felt a sharp push between my shoulderblades.

'Go on. Don't be shy.' Sophie gave me an extra shove.

Why I let myself be forced into such a silly ritual, I don't know. It wasn't as if I had any chance of getting married. I wasn't even playing the field.

I stood at the back of the swarm of singles.

The image of Rick Hunter came to mind. I could imagine all the sad single women at his wedding, staring on mournfully as he married the love of his life. His deep, dark eyes only for one woman. That hot body only for one wife. That deep velvety voice whispering sweet nothings only for her lucky ears.

The bouquet flew through the air.

It bounced off the heads of two squealing zealots, slipped through the fingers of a very large, very intimidating cousin, and slammed into my face.

My hands jerked. I caught the bouquet as it fell, my nose smarting, tears burning in my eyes, thanking the heavens it hadn't taken an eye out.

All the singles turned. Evil looks fell upon me. From Caitlin's cousin, especially.

'What a waste,' she bit out, flouncing her very full figure past me, knocking my shoulder and nearly sending me hurtling into the entwined lovers ice sculpture.

Was it a wake-up call?

I just stood there, gazing around the room in a daze, the bouquet clutched tightly to my breasts.

Was it a sign from God? Was Mr Right in the room, waiting?

I glanced around and every available guy in the room ducked for cover. Suddenly I was no longer just a good time waiting to happen. I was sizing them up for the old ball and chain—and the fear was stark in their eyes.

My mind jerked. This was *his* fault. If I'd had my mind on the bride, and not on Rick Hunter, I would've dodged the stupid bunch of flowers.

Caitlin shot me a grin.

I shook my head. No way. There was no way I was falling into that particular trap again—no way was I getting my hopes up. No way was I putting myself out there. Not a chance.

CHAPTER THREE

I SHOVED the key into my door and pushed it open, balancing the offending bunch of flowers in my arms. Okay, so I'd caught the bouquet—sort of. It was no big deal. It didn't mean anything. Not really. Besides, I was perfectly happy with my life.

I kicked my shoes off—they were killing me—and dropped my keys and handbag on the hall table. I could hear the fridge whirring away in the shadowy darkness.

A sigh escaped my lips and I let my shoulders slump. I was home—safe, quiet home.

I made my way to the freezer, where the choc-chip ice cream was beckoning me. Just what I needed to dull the echoes of people's comments at the reception. I swear I'd heard every possible witty-cum-sarcastic remark about bouquets, weddings and nuns.

The fridge door closed, but I barely heard it for the loud slurp of suction from the ice cream lid. I snatched up a spoon and ploughed in.

The rich, cold, creamy delight melted in my mouth, filling my senses. There was nothing quite like it. I scooped again. I was in no hurry. If it took all night to feel better—and/or to devour the whole tub—so be it…

I slid down the fridge door until my butt hit the cool, hard surface of the kitchen tiles, tears stinging behind my eyes. All women weren't created equal. Some fell into marriage with the most wonderful guy without any effort at all, while others—others were driven to dairy products.

I took another scoop, then stopped, spoon in mid-air, and tilted my head. Something was wrong. I couldn't put my finger on it. The place was just…different.

My stomach churned—and not just with the ice cream on top of the champagne on top of the chicken on top of the hors-d'oeuvres. But with the quick and disturbing realisation that I was not alone.

A noise erupted from the vicinity of the living room.

Sheer, black fright swept over me. I froze. My mind fluttered. Yes. There'd definitely been a noise in my apartment, but it could have been anything. It could have been George.

Fear knotted in my stomach. If it was George he'd find me any second now, nudging his wet nose against me for his share of the ice cream. I waited, holding my breath.

Silence. Absolute and utter silence.

My heart pounded in my chest. I covered my mouth to stifle the gasp tearing to escape from my lips. I had a burglar!

I placed the spoon carefully into the tub and set it very gently onto the tiled floor. I tried to keep control while panic welled inside me.

I stepped quietly, the ominous silence crawling up my spine. The shadowy apartment was menacing. He could be hiding in any shadow, in any corner. Why the hell hadn't I turned on the light?

All the horror movies I'd ever seen converged on me with frightful clarity—the victims in them never turned on the lights either!

I peered around the end of the kitchen bench, careful not to make a noise, half in anticipation of seeing George and feeling stupid, and half in dread.

I saw the silhouette against the window clearly. It wasn't George. He was big, probably brutish, and he was standing looking out towards Courtney's. Her lights were still on. He was either perving on her, or wondering where in hell I kept all my valuables.

My blood fired. I bit my lip. I was not going to be a victim. He was not going to take my hard-earned belongings just because he could.

I was on my feet in a milli-second. I reached out and found the frying pan I'd cooked yesterday's eggs in, still sitting on the stove. I could see the headline…*Woman foils burglary attempt with frying pan!* The accolade fired my body into action.

I lunged across the room, lifting the pan, swinging it back like a baseball bat, ready to swat the creep into next week.

He turned.

I gasped.

A strong hand grabbed my wrist, stopping my weapon's progress to his skull. A large foot hooked behind my legs, knocking them from under me. I fell.

The burglar pinned me to the floor with his hard, heavy body. A million images shot through my mind, none of them pleasant, fuelling my panic.

I kicked. I flailed. He held firm. I was getting nowhere. I went limp. I figured I was better off saving my energy for the right moment.

I sucked in a slow, deep breath. God, he smelled good…like exotic spices and potato crisps. And his body wasn't just heavy on mine, it was warm. How long had it been since I'd been this close to a male body? Obviously far too long. How could I be so desperate? I was fantasising about a burglar!

'Get off me, you creep!' I growled, my voice thick with fear.

He moved my hands together until he could use one of his to pin me to the floor and have the other

free. He patted me down, slapping the sides of my
body in a very efficient, methodical manner.
Doubts assailed me. I was getting the distinct impression he was about to tell me to 'spread them'.

He paused.

The blood raced through my body. I knew what
was coming and I wasn't going to let it happen. I
felt him shift his weight.

The light flicked on, blinding me. I jerked my
knee with all the ferocity I could muster—thinking
of my ex-boyfriends lent me an untapped energy I
wish I'd found sooner.

The burglar gasped as my knee connected with
his family jewels.

I blinked until I could see through the glare.

Rick Hunter lay on top of me, his hand gripping
the edge of the table where the lamp sat as though
he was trying to break a piece off, his face set, his
eyes fiery.

'What the hell are you doing here?' There was
a definite tremor in my voice and I hated myself
for the weakness.

'I moved…in today,' he said through gritted
teeth.

I opened my mouth, but no words came out.

He took several deep, gasping breaths. 'You
weren't here. I waited…an hour. You didn't come.
I got Alan. He opened…your door.'

His face was only inches from mine. And his eyes weren't dark; they were the deepest blue I'd ever seen. I swallowed. What did one say in a situation like this?

'Well, I do have a life,' I bit out defensively. 'You didn't tell me *when* you were moving in.'

'I thought…it was obvious…that I…wanted to move in…right away.'

'No, it wasn't.' I was suddenly very aware of his warm, hard body against mine. His hand was still pinning me to the floor—and believe me, it wasn't an altogether unpleasant experience.

My heart hammered, my pulse pounded, and the pit of my stomach ached. For more.

I tried to throttle the dizzying current racing through my veins. This was detrimental to my new-found immunity to men. 'You can get off me now,' I bit out, trying to sound calm.

He hesitated, looking into my eyes, then dropped his gaze to my creamy shoulders, then down my body.

My heart lurched and the ripple of excitement was almost too much to bear. But the agony was ecstasy, in a masochistic sort of way. He was married, after all. I meant nothing to him.

Rick rolled off me. 'I didn't hurt you, did I?'

I couldn't watch him straighten and get to his feet. I hoped I hadn't hurt *him* too badly. What a way to start sharing a place with someone. Though a great way to give them the hint that you didn't want them there!

I moved quickly, picking up the frying pan and striding to the safety of the kitchen. If I was lucky he'd leave it be and I wouldn't have to explain myself—or apologise for the injury and have to think about that certain part of his anatomy.

'You should get lessons in self-defence.' His words were as cool as ice.

I stiffened. Trust a guy to have to have the last word. 'I already *have* had lessons.' I dropped the pan in the sink full of dishes. 'Thank you very much.'

'And they taught you to go after burglars with a frying pan?'

I spun around. 'No, they taught me to kick your—' I clattered some dishes for impact. 'Which, by the way, I did. Which, by the way, did disable you. Which, by the way, would have been just as efficient had you *really* been an intruder.'

Rick rubbed his neck and shook his head, walking stiffly towards the kitchen—and me—his eyes glinting as though he wanted to show me exactly what might have happened. 'That's not enough. You could just fuel the guy's anger.'

He stopped at the sofa and gripped the back of the headrest tightly. 'And, by the way, you wouldn't have had a chance to do it if I hadn't been reaching for the light-switch. Which a real intruder wouldn't have done.'

Heat flooded my cheeks. He was right, and the thought was as uncomfortable as his preaching. Damn him.

'You panicked,' Rick accused, his voice laced with cool authority.

I stood silent for a second. 'Of course I panicked. I thought you were a burglar.' He'd sneaked around as if he was a burglar. 'Why on earth *were* you wandering around in the dark?'

Rick stared at me, his deep blue eyes sliding over my body as though he was looking at me for the first time. 'I…had trouble finding the light-switch.'

I was suddenly very aware that I was wearing the peach dress *again*. He'd think I lived in the thing. I crossed my arms over my chest. 'You were right next to the lamp,' I accused—which he'd managed to find while he was struggling with me on the floor!

He crossed his arms over his chest. 'I was in the dark because I was taking a moment.'

'O-kay.' It was probably far more polite to say that than to admit perving on Courtney.

I moved to see what she was doing across the way. My foot connected with the tub of ice cream. I paused. I'd rather have gone to hell and back than picked it up and put it back in the fridge with Rick standing there. He didn't need to know about my vice. I glanced out of the window. Courtney Jenkins was sitting on the sofa watching TV. Big thrill.

'Well, I'm sorry for…' My eyes dropped to the area in question. I couldn't wait for him to apologise. What would he say? Would he say sorry for dropping me to the ground, pinning me to the floor with his hard, hot body? Or just for smelling like heaven on earth? I stifled the thought.

Rick waved a hand dismissively. He looked as if he was struggling to find words. 'Goodnight,' he finally said. And he was gone. He closed the door to the spare room with finality.

Anger rippled up my spine and through my veins. He could have said sorry. I rubbed my butt, which had taken the brunt of the fall, and stuck my tongue out at his door. But I didn't feel any better. He was just too cool for my own good.

I shoved the ice cream tub back in the freezer, thanking the heavens I'd survived that little interlude with my dignity somewhat intact. So I'd nearly concussed my new boarder. So, I'd had my self-defence skills summarily squashed, and been floored. So I'd had a rush of feelings in places I'd long forgotten existed. I had come out okay. I was in control.

So he hadn't said he was sorry—I wasn't sorry he was gone. I couldn't have kept up the conversation. All I could think about was how nice his body had felt against mine. And I knew—every inch of my body knew—Rick Hunter was a test I wasn't ready for.

I stared at the rather bruised bouquet, lying discarded on the bench. It meant nothing. And neither did my racing pulse and hot face. Nothing at all.

The morning sun brought a new mood. I was over it. Over him. Over everything. It was just that one thing had added to another. Overwhelmed, that was what I'd been.

Having Rick Hunter in my apartment wasn't a big deal at all. I was a more mature, more grounded person than I'd ever been and I could handle him. No worries.

I sipped my cup of coffee, nice and strong and bolstering. There was no reason to think I couldn't handle him. Besides, if I put my brain to work I was sure to figure out some way to get rid of the guy.

'What's this?' Rick's velvet-smooth voice cut through my thoughts.

I looked up from my magazine, ready for whatever Rick Hunter was going to throw at my convictions today.

My breath froze in my throat.

Rick stood in the doorway, dripping with water, his bronzed body interrupted only by a towel around his hips.

His appeal was devastating. His arms were strongly muscled, his shoulders wide, his chest solid, scattered with dark curls of hair that trailed a line down his flat stomach to the towel. And his legs…long and tanned—and as damned nice as the rest of him.

Every nerve in my body lurched in excitement. My blood heated and the urge to stand up, strip off and join him was almost too much to resist. I bit my finger, hoping the pain would bring me to my senses. It didn't. I couldn't tear my eyes away from him.

'Well?' Rick's deep tones reverberated through me. 'What's this?'

I swallowed hard. 'A naked man?'

His forehead creased and his eyes narrowed. 'No. Yes.' His lips quirked, as though they were fighting a smile. 'But I meant this.' Rick waved his hand in the air.

I forced myself to focus on it and not the body attached to it. He had something in his hand. Recognition dawned. 'Oh.'

'Yes—oh. Now, would you like to explain why there's a turtle in your bath?'

I was so embarrassed I wanted to hide. But instead I sucked in a deep, calming breath and shrugged. What could I say? It was self-explanatory. 'He lives there.'

'And did this little critter come with the apartment, or is he another one of your strays?'

'What do you think?' My blood was already hot, but now in anger. Al had obviously filled him in on the rumours—or on his suspicions. Was this guy really a cousin or was he a spy? Or both!

I stood up, stomped up to him and plucked Caesar from his hand, trying very hard to ignore the close proximity of his very naked, very male, very perfect body. 'Caesar isn't a critter. He's a turtle. And he doesn't like being waved around.'

I glared up at Rick. How dared he call them strays? How dared he waltz around the apartment mostly naked? How dared he talk to me like this? How dared he spy on me? And to call Caesar 'little' was only going to add to his complex. He was going to be a great big tough turtle…one day.

Rick looked down into my eyes.

My pulse skipped, but I glared up at him, projecting what I hoped was pure and utter confidence. I mentally dared him to go running to Al about the turtle.

'I think you're pushing it.'

What, I had no idea. And I didn't want to know. I was barely a foot away from the most perfect male body in the state. I met his glare. His deepest, bluest eyes held mine and a sensuous light passed between us. Time stopped. All there was was me, Rick's deep blue eyes and Caesar, squirming in my hand.

'You're one crazy lady, you know that.' And he swung around, stalked back into the bathroom and slammed the door.

He only knew the half of it.

I put Caesar in my empty cereal bowl on the table, and collapsed into a chair. I dropped my head onto the table with a satisfying thud.

There was no use denying it. Seventeen months of being celibate was too long. I clenched my hands into fists and struggled against the waves of desire washing through my body. It was over. But I had learnt a lot.

Going without had given me a new appreciation for the joys of a relationship. As had the married, off-limits, seriously sexy Mr Hunter. I wasn't going to miss out on the joys of a relationship, ever again.

I didn't want to be a nun.

I didn't want to be alone.

I didn't want to find new friends.

I didn't want to feel like this around the very married, very unsuitable Rick Hunter.

I wanted one nice, normal, safe, average-looking man. I wasn't looking for Mr Perfect, I just wanted Mr Right.

I stood up, skittling my chair. It was time to get serious. I was ready to cultivate cast-iron balls and stick myself squarely back in the dating wars...

So, the chances of dating a stalker, kissing a loser or, worse, getting stuck with another blind date seemed to outweigh the possibility of finding Mr Right. But it didn't have to be that way.

I could find Mr Right. I wasn't young and naïve any more. I wasn't being driven by desperation or by rebound. I was going to do it properly this time. No flying by the seat of my pants. This time...I was going to be smart.

I was going to have nothing to do with drop-dead gorgeous hunks who had the tendency to fall out of love as quickly as they fell in. Who had sexy-as-hell mouths that lied as easily as they whispered sweet nothings. Who had deep, dark eyes that scored my soul as easily as they wandered off with others.

I was going to find a nice safe, quiet gentleman to settle down with and live happily ever after. Or cry trying.

CHAPTER FOUR

SOPHIE and I usually meet on Wednesdays for lunch at a café in Richmond, where I work—but I couldn't wait that long. I'd braved the city in lunch-hour madness to meet her at a trendy little café tucked in an alley. Frantic shoppers and suits made their way past, dodging the tables, chairs and diners on the walkway. Luckily, Sophie had secured a table inside.

'So, you're on the market again?'

I nodded, sitting down to my café latte with a sinking feeling in the pit of my stomach. Did I really want this? Was I ready for another bout of dating? I was ready—more than ready—to find Mr Right, but I'd so much rather wake up one morning with him magically beside me.

Sophie clapped her hands together in front of her, her smile threatening to tear her cheeks. 'And you want *my* help. I knew it. All this new-fangled find-yourself rubbish has nothing on a good—'

'I get it.' I didn't really want to hear anything more about what I'd been missing out on. My body had been aching all day, in all sorts of places, and my mind was indelibly scored with Rick's near-naked body. And I hated him for it. How dared he blackmail his way into my apartment and turn my safe, comfortable life upside down? I would just have to return the favour…

'So, are you after the same sort of guy as last time?'

'Which was?' I couldn't even remember what I'd asked for, or if I *had* asked for any sort of guy in particular. It had been so long ago…

'Anything male!' She laughed.

I couldn't even smile. This was no joking matter. I swallowed the dull ache in my throat, focussing on what good could come. 'I have worked out a few things while I've been on my sabbatical. I want a quiet, conservative, responsible sort of guy.' That I did know. 'And I'm looking for a tall, dark and okay-looking man—*not* handsome—with a nice smile and a deep, smooth voice.'

'But is he looking for you?'

I leant back in my chair and crossed my arms, shooting her a black look. 'Sophie, I'm serious. I need to find Mr Right.'

'You *really* want to do the blind dates again?' She bit her lip. 'You're really serious and not just kidding me?'

'Yes.' I didn't care whether it was another dreaded blind date, or ten. At least then someone knew the guy, could vouch that he wasn't some psycho nutcase or an ex-con. Or married.

'Okay.' She waved her pastry in the air. 'Mark knows some other accountants. They're pretty conservative.'

Mark was Sophie's hubby and had so many mates and work contacts that Sophie had sworn she could keep me blind dating for years.

I cringed. The idea of blind dates was so distasteful, so bloody hard on the self-esteem—you virtually screamed 'loser' by accepting one. You almost guaranteed that the guy would be too. And, in this case, two negatives didn't make a positive.

But I wasn't about to do the club scene again. That had ended in disaster time and again. Okay, so it had taken me longer than the average woman to surrender to the fact that I'm hopeless at choosing men. But even I had to concede after Alex.

'Fine. Accountants sound fine. As long as they're under thirty-five and don't have a criminal record.' I swallowed hard, welling up my courage. 'I'm game.'

'Terrific.' She nodded enthusiastically for a minute, then slowed the bob of her head until she stared me in the eye. 'But what I don't get is why you've changed your mind all of a sudden.'

'I just can't see myself being alone any more.' I stirred my coffee again, trying not to think of how wonderfully tanned Rick Hunter's muscles were—all over. Of how his deep blue eyes twinkled, or of how his voice slid over me like lotion.

'Can you get me a blind date for tonight?' I blurted.

Sophie bit into her chocolate éclair. 'Why the rush?'

I gnawed on my lower lip, wondering whether I should confess my attraction for the perfect male body of my new flatmate.

'It's that new guy you've let the room to, isn't it? I can't wait to meet him.' Sophie's eyes gleamed as only a married matchmaker's could.

'I can't wait to get rid of him,' I shot back, driving home to her exactly where I stood. 'A month. I have to put up with him for a whole month.'

She ignored me. 'He's writing a book, right? What's it about?' She raised her voice over the din of the peak-hour crowd in the coffee shop.

'Torturing young single women, no doubt.' I stared into my double latte dolefully. I hadn't been able to stop thinking about him. The jerk. Two days and he'd already managed to screw with my mind. The din softened.

'You're just desperate, that's all.' Sophie's voice boomed out. A dozen heads turned in our direction and my face heated swiftly. 'How long has it been since you've had a good old-fashioned—?'

'Thank you.' I grabbed Sophie's arm, silencing her. I didn't want the entire place to know that I'd chickened out of dating any more disasters, or how long it had been since I was with a guy. 'It's been a while, okay,' I whispered harshly. 'And I'm not desperate. I'm just keen.'

'Okay. So, are you *keen* on your new flatmate?'

'Definitely not. He's…totally not what I'm after.'

Trust Sophie to forget about subtlety, politeness and tact and just say it. I had no idea if I sounded convincing—but by the look on her face I guess I could have done with several days' rehearsing.

'Okay, if you say so.' Sophie sipped her tea, shooting me a coy look. 'So how goes this sharing with a *stranger*?'

'He's a cousin of Al's. He's not exactly a stranger.' I knew where she was heading, and I was not going to contemplate clubs again. Strangers were out.

'And you don't think Al's relative could be dangerous?'

That was a good point. Just because I knew Al—and I have to say here that he's not the nicest cup in the cupboard—it didn't guarantee anything. But from what little I already knew of Rick Hunter, what I felt about Rick Hunter, he wasn't dangerous in that way. He was dangerous in another way entirely.

I closed my eyes and saw his seriously sexy body taunting me again. My nerves tingled, my blood heated and my body ached. And *that* was scarier than any criminal record.

Sophie pushed her blonde hair back from her face. 'Maybe I should come and meet him so I can identify him in a line-up if they find you all—'

'Sophie!' I shook my head. 'He's not like that. It's not like that. Cripes. You'll give me nightmares.' And my mind darted to how nicely Rick Hunter could sneak into my nightmares and wreak havoc…

Sophie put up her palms in front of her. 'Okay, I'll stop. But I just wanted to see if you've contemplated what sort of person you're sharing your place with.'

I'd done that, all right. I'd contemplated all sorts of things with Rick Hunter…

'I mean, do you really know who he is? What he's doing?'

'Sure,' I lied. He was married, and that was all I'd contemplated. Apart from a tantalising fantasy of him not being tied to a woman that was 'perfect'. And strangling the annoying jerk. 'I don't know what you're getting so serious about. All I want is a date.'

She raised one of her finely shaped eyebrows. 'Why now?'

I could have told her that it was because Rick Hunter was flaunting his perfect body in front of me, taunting me with what I'd been missing out on. But I didn't. There were some things I just didn't feel comfortable sharing with my friends— like how pathetically desperate I was. 'I'm sick of being single.'

'The grass is always greener...'

'Well, I can't wait to move to other pastures.'

'You're just saying that. You'll miss the dating scene once you're hitched.' Sophie leant back and stared out of the window at the passing people.

I shook my head. Maybe on my silver anniversary...

'Look, I've got to go.' Sophie stood up, casting a long look at her watch. 'I'll call you about your date, okay?'

'Are you sure you can't get one for tonight?' Anything had to be better than contemplating another night in with Rick, alone.

She shrugged. 'Not a chance.'

I watched her leave, her words sinking in. I was going to be alone with Rick Hunter tonight. A shiver ran down my spine and every tingling nerve in my body knew it wasn't a good idea. It was a bad idea. Very, very bad.

I stared around the café mournfully, willing my brain to come up with some solution. I could go out with one of the girls, if anyone could get away from her hubby and didn't have anything else on. I cringed. It would be obvious that I was desperate for company and I didn't want that. I wasn't desperate for company. I was desperate to avoid Rick Hunter. There was a big difference.

The movies were an option. Or there'd be a play on somewhere, or a show. But there'd be nothing comparable to walking out of my door, away from Rick, with a man at my side.

I couldn't help but notice that there were three very nice-looking guys seated near the door. They were all dressed in suits, clean-shaven and smart-looking.

I sighed. There had to be an easy way to meet nice guys. I wondered how Rick had met his wife…

There was a chance Rick's wife would turn up for a visit—maybe even tonight. My stomach clenched tight. I could imagine how they missed each other.

I stood abruptly and strode over to the men.

'Hi…' I faltered. What could I possibly say that didn't sound dorky or desperate? 'Would one of you lovely gentlemen be able to tell me how to get to the Grand Central station?' I mentally crossed my fingers. How stupid did that sound?

The cute-looking one closest to me ran his gaze over me. I held my breath, my breasts growing in size.

'I can do more than that for you. I can escort you there. It's only a block away,' he said with ease.

'Thank you, that'd be great.'

Score! I let him guide me out of the café to the hoots of his mates.

I had learnt something while out of the game. What? I had no idea, but my luck had definitely changed. Maybe my luck batteries had been re-charged by celibacy…?

'The city can be a bit overwhelming if you don't have a map,' he offered.

I walked beside him, wondering what the hell I was doing. This was exactly what I hadn't wanted—a total stranger! I rallied my strength. I could do this. 'I don't know what I would've done if you hadn't come along.' I glanced at my watch. 'I have an appointment.' And I needed to get back to work.

'I'll get you there.' He smiled at me.

I pasted a smile on my face. 'Thanks.' To think all I had to do was have the confidence to pander to a man's 'knight' complex and *bam*, I had him by the—

'Here we are. See, no drama at all.'

I turned to face him. 'Thank you so much for your help. I'm so grateful. My name's Casey.' I stuck out my hand. 'Casey Wilson.' There was no way I was letting him go without committing him-self to seeing me tonight.

'Steven Rodderman.' He wrapped his hand around mine and cast me an appreciative smile, as though he'd just realised that it was more than just directions I wanted from him.

I waited, content for him to shake my hand and look me over again. He wouldn't have a problem. I was looking great in my work gear. I wore a short grey skirt and a fitted white shirt. Luckily I was minus the apron I put on when I'm working with the animals.

'I was wondering—would you like to have a drink with me some time?' he said casually, his tone gentle.

I bit my lip to stifle a whoop of victory. 'I'm awfully busy, Steven,' I said slowly, forcing a relaxed calm into my voice.

I could see his shoulders slumping.

'But I am free tonight.'

He shot me a smile. 'Tonight it is, then. Do you want to meet me somewhere, or can I pick you up?'

A vision of Steven coming to my door and picking me up invaded my mind. Walking through the door with him and leaving the annoying Rick Hunter behind. It would be nice. It would be more than nice. It would be perfect.

I yanked a pen out of my bag and scribbled my address and phone number on it. I handed it to him. 'Later.' And I managed the sort of smile I hadn't given a guy in a very long time.

'See you later.' He waved me off, beaming.

I went into the station just as thrilled. I wasn't going to have to put up with Rick Hunter tonight. I was going on a date. And it was going to be *so good*…

No more creeps for me. No more disasters. And Sophie was right. I shouldn't take Mr Hunter for granted either. I should find out exactly who he was, then make my own decisions. Just as I had with Steven.

I smiled all the way back to work. I'm in control. I'm powerful. I'm *the* woman!

I stepped out of the shower, smiling at my reflection in the foggy mirror. I'd found my inner bitch. I'd heard finding one's inner bitch was a must on the dating scene. If you didn't have that tough self-assurance you were better off out of the madness. And I'd found it. I'd *finally* found it!

I slung my dressing gown around my damp body. I had a million things to do. I had to find the right outfit. I had to do my hair. My nails, my face…

When I'd arrived home the first thing I'd taken note of was the silence. Then I'd checked, just in case Rick was skulking around and about to mistake me for a burglar. But Rick was out.

The peal of the phone made me jump.

I picked it up. 'Hello—Casey Wilson.' I crossed my fingers that it was more good news.

'Casey. It's me—Sophie. Have I got the dream man for you. He's thirty, six feet tall, with an income that ensures you'd get your little house in the 'burbs, with a white picket fence, two kids and a dog.'

'I have a dog.'

'I know you have a dog. It's just a saying.'

'When?' I crossed my fingers it wasn't going to be tonight. That would be a cruel twist. No dates for almost one and a half years, then two dates in one night.

'That's the best part. Tomorrow night. You're to meet him at that French restaurant down on the Southbank.'

Tomorrow. That didn't leave me much time. An accountant. I'd have to look the part for an accountant. I'd have to lose three kilos, find a knock-'em-dead outfit, get my hair cut and get a bit organised.

'What's his name?' Always a good thing to note, to save you from asking every guy in the place if he was your date. This I'd learnt from experience.

'Anthony Calahan.'

He sounded perfect. Could a girl tell from a name if the man was meant for her? I hoped so. I needed this guy to be Mr Right. I was through with the wrong type of guys. I was through with being alone. I was through with shopping and cooking for one.

And who could forget cute-looking Steven from the café? My saviour for the night. He could be the one…

I rang off.

I ran a hand over my thighs, noticing how my Saturday-night movies had affected my figure. A packet of chocolate biscuits and a few glasses of wine each week had really put it on.

I strode across the lounge to grab an apple from the fruit bowl. I bit down into the crisp skin, staring out of the window. Courtney was out. Her lights were all off. I smiled. Maybe she'd found someone to date tonight too. Hopefully he was a nice guy and not some stalker.

I glanced to the spare bedroom and my mind went into overdrive. Sophie was right. I knew nothing about Rick Hunter.

Okay, so call me suicidal—or just stupid. But I wasn't going to let my mind come up with a zillion crazy options for what he might have in his room.

It was my place. I had a right to know. Curiosity had nothing to do with it. I pushed open the door and flicked the light-switch.

A camp mattress was blown up and pushed against one wall, with a sleeping bag neatly spread on top and all sorts of stuff beside it: water bottle, notepads, torch, camera, binoculars.

I glanced through a gap in the curtains and saw that Courtney was coming in the door with her son. My chest ached for her. I'd really thought she might have had a date. She'd been alone for as long as I could remember her being there.

I moved further into the room. Rick's laptop was set up on the dresser that Caitlin had left behind. The screen was up, and a small light shone from the top of the keyboard. It was on. Would he mind if I just sneaked a peek? He didn't seem the sort of guy who was into sharing, and if I was ever going to read a bit of his book…

I moved over to the dresser, my eyes firmly fixed on the screen, willing it to blink on without me having to go across the entire room. My mind went into overdrive. What was he writing? A dry text or an autobiography? A thriller or a juicy mystery?

I reached out, my finger stretched, reaching for the touch-pad. I was dying to read what he was laying out in words in a book—I might find something seriously revealing about him.

'What the hell are you doing in here?' Rick's voice was unmistakable. And there was no doubt from his tone—he was livid!

CHAPTER FIVE

I SWUNG around, willing my cheeks to stay cool, my voice to stay calm. I opened my mouth. I had trespassed in his personal space. And from the look in his eyes I was about to face the music. I sucked in air.

'Just checking you had everything you need,' I blurted, my heart pounding. 'Obviously you don't. I have a spare bed down in the basement storage that you could use while you're here, and a few other things. I even have a desk, if you want it. I didn't realise you were roughing it. Or was that your intention? Part of the research for your book? Is it fiction or true?'

Verbal diarrhoea only attacks when I'm nervous. And nervous was an understatement. Rick advanced on me like a fox on a chicken and I took a deep breath, ready to let loose some more good reasons for snooping, but the words stuck in my throat at the look in his eyes.

Intense, flaming blue eyes raked my body as he reduced the distance between us. I clutched my dressing gown tighter around myself, very aware that I was totally naked underneath.

He pulled himself up centimetres from me. I was enveloped in a cloud of his scent. Cologne mixed with pure and utter male sweat.

'The elevator's not working?' I had the stupidity to ask.

His mouth thinned. 'I was in a hurry. Didn't use it.'

'Why?' My voice came out small, squeaky. My lips were dry. I wanted to swallow. I wanted to lick them, but I couldn't. Not with Rick Hunter staring at me as though I was an alien intruder. 'Your wife coming?'

A shadow passed over his eyes, wiping the anger from them. 'No.' He ran a hand through his hair and stalked to the window, staring out.

'Well, I'd love to stay and chat, but I'm very busy. Let me know if you need those things from storage…' I headed towards my room in what I hoped wasn't a run but should have been.

'I want to talk to you,' he barked, his voice demanding compliance.

I balked. I'm not into compliance, and I wasn't ready to get barrelled over intruding on his space. I kept walking.

'Hey.'

I swung around. 'Hey, yourself. You push your way into my place and expect me to merrily accept you as my roomie? I think not. And if I felt in any way insecure about a stranger in my place, and went to find out more about you, do you blame me?'

'You could just ask me.'

'And what gives you the idea that I'd accept anything you say at face value?' I bit my tongue. Damn. I hadn't meant to say that out loud.

'You think I'd lie to you?' He sounded surprised.

I was sick of pussyfooting around. 'In a word—yes.'

He shifted on his feet. 'That's a pretty cynical view. Is it just me, or the world in general that has you believing no one is to be trusted?'

'Yes.'

'To which one?'

'Pick one.' I spun on my heel and walked off, slamming my bedroom door to emphasise the end of the conversation. I hated the man! He was the most irritating human being I'd ever met. How on earth could he get on my nerves so easily? Why did I let him?

I yanked open my cupboard and started pulling clothes out. I wasn't going to give Rick Hunter another thought. I was going to focus on my date. The very helpful Steven. I smiled, willing my pulse to quieten. I couldn't wait until he arrived.

My black dress was perfect for tonight. Elegant, yet not overdone. I glanced around. The entire contents of my wardrobe were littered around the room. I shrugged. Sacrifices had to be made.

I heard the knock at the front door. I smiled. Rick could answer it and entertain Steven while I finished getting ready.

I slipped on the black dress. Rick would get Steven a drink, just as Caitlin used to do for my visitors, ages ago now, chatting with them until I was ready.

I coated my eyelashes with mascara, intent on my reflection in the dresser's mirror. A movement caught my eye.

Rick leant in the doorway. How long he'd been there, I didn't know. And how had he opened the door without me hearing? I'd assumed he would be talking to Steve in the lounge.

'There's a guy on the doorstep for you.' He filled the doorway, his muscular body hugged by a sweatshirt, his blue denims tight on him, and a power coiled within him that was as stirring as his compelling blue eyes.

My pulse skittered. My heart pounded. My cheeks heated. My body warmed. I focused on his words. 'You could invite him in.'

'I don't know the guy. Do you?' His voice was soft, deep and challenging.

I stiffened. 'As a matter of fact, yes,' I lied. I wasn't about to suffer another lecture from Rick.

I dabbed my lips with a rich blood-red, watching his reflection as much as I was watching mine.

He shoved his hands deep in his pockets. 'Can you leave me his full name and contact details?'

I swung around to face him. 'Why?' I slashed the brush through my brown hair again.

'Didn't they teach you anything in that self-defence class?' His tone was firm, serious. 'So someone knows where you've gone and who with.'

I crossed my arms in front of me. 'Who made you my keeper?'

He shrugged.

'Can you go invite Steven in, please?'

Rick shook his head. 'Can't.'

'And why is that?'

'Because the place is a mess.'

I bit my lip. I couldn't argue with him on that one. I cast a quick look around at the debris of my preparations—what must he think of this place? But Rick wasn't looking at the mess...

Rick was looking at me. And not just looking at me. He was *looking at me*. My pulse skittered as his eyes slid slowly up from my black heels to my stockinged legs—which gave me a lovely tan I would've killed for—then up over my knees to my form-fitting black dress—which looked pretty good on me. His eyes rested momentarily on my breasts. A fair swell of them were on display, thanks to the low-cut neck.

I held my breath.

His gaze went up to my freshly coloured lips and then met my green eyes. My heart danced in excitement. My cheeks heated under my make-up and my breath was ragged. My nerves were all standing on end, beckoning him to do with his lips and hands what he'd evoked with his eyes.

How could he make me feel so much with just a look? I shivered. How dared he look at me like this? He was married! 'Have you quite finished?'

He blinked and swallowed, as though he didn't understand what I'd said.

'You are married, you know.'

He crossed his arms over his chest, stifling the look. 'I am a guy, you know.'

'That doesn't give you an excuse.'

'I was only looking.'

'Well, don't.'

Tension zinged between us. I glared at him. He stared back, as though he was ready to say something really important…

'I want to talk to you about privacy.'

That was great—after he'd looked at me so thoroughly I felt I needed to have a cigarette. I turned back to my mirror. 'Talk.'

'I just wanted to say—'

I smoothed out the creases in my dress, running my hands down my hips and wriggling the wrinkles out of my stockings.

'I want to say that—'

I tilted my head and rubbed perfume on one side, then the other, touching my pulse-points with the scent.

'That my room is my space—'

I fluffed my hair up, combing it with my fingers to give it a natural look, and adjusted the neckline of my dress again so my breasts weren't as exposed.

'That my space is off-limits.'

I turned. I was glad getting ready had taken me so long. Rick had cooled off about my trespass to the point of vagueness. I couldn't feel anything behind his words. But his eyes—his eyes were glued to me.

I willed my body to behave and my heart to slow. It was no big deal. 'No problem. Can you tell Steven I'll be out in a minute?' I surprised myself with how normal I sounded, and started fussing with my dress again—the stupid thing was riding up. Anything was better than looking at Rick staring at me.

'You look great,' Rick murmured softly, then coughed and left.

I stared at the empty doorway. Coming from Rick Hunter I should have been thrilled. I wasn't. I was scared.

I stood at my doorway on the landing and just stared at it, then at my watch—it wasn't even nine o'clock—then I looked at the door again and sighed heavily.

The date had been a disaster. Steven had taken me to a bar seven blocks away—I know; I counted each one as I trudged back. He'd ordered our drinks and then stared wholly and unerringly at my breasts.

I'd tried to talk to him—about anything, about everything, the weather, the economy, himself—to no avail.

He wasn't as tall as I'd remembered him—I must have been wearing my flats earlier, and tonight, in heels, my breasts had been on his eye level. I'd thought I could handle his adoration for my attributes, but when a woman passed with a pair of double Ds I'd lost his attention completely.

I leant back against the wall, blinking back the dry ache in my throat. It was the first time my cleavage had been dumped for a better cup.

So much for my inner bitch and my good luck.

The second hand on my watch passed slowly. Too slowly. I shifted on my feet. At least I had Anthony's date tomorrow to hang on to. I sucked in a deep breath. I couldn't get excited about the prospect, even if he turned out to be Mr Right. It was all too scary even to think about.

My door opened.

I plunged my hand into my bag for my keys, trying to get my feet back into my heels and do my best to look as if I'd just arrived. All the while my cheeks were blazing with a burning heat that Rick couldn't help but notice.

'What are you doing?' Rick asked.

'Just finding my keys.' I stretched my toes, chasing my right shoe—it wasn't behaving. I couldn't get my toes into it and I was painfully aware that he was watching. I bent down, snatched it up, and strode past Rick Hunter into my apartment.

'You were standing on the doorstep.'

I dropped the shoe onto the hall stand with my purse and kicked the other one off. 'And if I was? Is there a law against that?'

'Your date didn't work out?' Rick closed the door and leant against it, his gentle tone washing over me.

'He…he got called away. Urgent business.' I struggled out of my jacket and draped it over the hall stand, unable to look Rick in the eyes for the lie.

'What does he do?'

'No idea.' I strode to the kitchen. I needed a stiff shot of chocolate, and fast. I hesitated at the fridge door. It wasn't something I did in front of guys.

Rick followed. 'You didn't ask what he did?'

'I don't care, okay.' I gave the freezer a long, hard look, then kept moving—there was no way I could gorge on double choc-chip ice cream with Rick watching.

'Okay.' He leant back onto the kitchen bench. 'Though I would like to add that if the man had been some maniac I could have done with his details.'

I swung to face him. 'So you could work out where the body was buried? Thanks for your consideration.' The words burst from my mouth. Why on earth had Rick opened the door? I could have done with some more space—heaps more.

'He didn't see you home, I take it?'

'No.' I stared at the bench. Why couldn't Rick just leave me alone? It wasn't as if he was the date police. I wanted to forget the night had ever happened. Though it did drive home the fact that I couldn't pick up a stranger in a café and expect a happy-ever-after.

'He doesn't sound like a responsible sort of man at all. That's not the sort of guy you can rely on to be a loving partner, let alone a good father to your children.'

'Sheesh, it was just one date.' I gave Rick a dark look. 'Thank you for your wisdom, but you're not my big brother. Far from it.'

He crossed his arms over his formidable chest. 'You're not seeing him again?'

I tilted my head. Why did he care? 'No. Not that it's any of your business, because it's not.' My throat tightened.

Rick appeared relieved.

'But I've got a date tomorrow night,' I bit out.

I don't know why I told him. Maybe to drum home to him that I wasn't a total loser. I don't know. He made me so damned confused. 'With someone else,' I shot at him.

Coffee. I needed coffee. I flicked the switch on the kettle and lurched towards the sink. No cups. I scanned the surface of the bench. No dishes. I glanced to the table. There had to be one there…I'd used three yesterday. Or was that the same one thrice?

'They're in the cupboard.'

Rick's velvety smooth voice slipped through me. I could barely discern the words. My mind grappled to understand. 'What?'

'Everything.'

I stared at the bench—tidy. I stared at the sink—empty and shining. I stared at the table—all neat and organised—with a tablecloth! Where had he found *that*?

I met his smiling eyes. 'You cleaned!' My insides curled. God, I hated him. 'How dare you clean up my mess?'

Rick broke into a smile. 'Since I live here, it's sort of my mess too.'

I opened my mouth, but no words came out. His smile was devastating. It shone from his eyes. It softened his features. It melted me…

'A thank-you would be great,' he offered lightly.

I opened my mouth—it would, in normal circumstances—but I couldn't get any words out. It was sweet. It was a lovely gesture. It was amazing that he could do so easily what I hated to do so much.

But I'd rather visit hell than admit that Rick had done me any sort of favour. It wasn't a favour, anyway. It was just a way for him to make me feel…like this. Small. Sloppy. Sizzling with sensation!

Rick dropped his arms and held the bench on either side of him. 'I think you have a rodent problem in the pantry.'

I crossed my arms and gave him the best imitation of wide-eyed concern that I could muster, pleased that this was one thing I could definitely handle. 'I do, do I? Why do you think that?'

'I heard noises in there.'

I glanced at my walk-in pantry and suppressed a smile. 'What do you suggest?' I asked innocently. It was time to win back a few points…

'Bait. Or a trap.' Rick shrugged.

'But how will I know which if I don't know what's in there? It could be a cockroach, a possum, or a teensy-weensy little mouse for all I know.'

Rick sucked in his breath, shot me an assessing glance, then opened the pantry door and stepped in.

I held my breath. I watched him climb the shelves, giving each one a thorough search as he went, my anticipation agony. This was going to be so good.

'There—something moved,' he whispered. 'Oh, my…what the…? Casey!' Rick dropped to the floor and faced me, his face not as pale and meek as I'd wished it to be but just the opposite—flushed and fierce.

My body shivered at my name on his lips—or was it the fire in his eyes. 'What? Oh, you mean Waldo's *in there*?' I tried my best at sounding innocent.

He crossed his arms over his chest. 'If Waldo is a two-metre-long python, then, yes, Waldo is in there.' Rick ran a hand through his dark hair, and from the look on his face I could tell that he knew I'd known and was actually impressed. 'You surprise me.'

I shot him a smile of my own.

Rick stiffened, staring at me. 'My cousin's not going to like this...Alan hates snakes.'

I'd forgotten all about Al—and the fact that Rick was his sly, snooping cousin. What had I done? I closed my eyes and centred my thoughts, but I couldn't ignore my nagging curiosity. 'Are *you* scared of snakes?'

He ran his hand over his chin. 'You know, guys like knowing what they're getting into when they date a woman.'

'Are you saying guys won't like me if I surprise them with my little family of pets?' I challenged, my blood firing at his suggestion. 'Do *you* like me, knowing about them?'

'I...I'm...' He straightened and backed away. 'I'm married. I don't count.'

'That's not an answer,' I blurted, biting my tongue. But I wished I hadn't even asked. I didn't want his opinion on anything—let alone on me. I wanted him gone.

'All I'm saying is that if you want a man to love you for who you are, you have to show him who you are—not this.' He waved a hand down at my dress.

I bit my lip. 'It's just a dress.'

'It's an advertisement.'

'Really? Of what?'

'That you're ready, willing and eager to please.'

'Really?' My blood heated. 'I see it as good manners to dress nicely—and, believe it or not, this is nicely.' It wasn't as if I was wearing a short red mini-skirt and a sequinned boob-tube.

'Then we'll have to agree to disagree.' Rick spun on his heel and strode to his bedroom door. 'But until you bring home a man and introduce him to your menagerie you'll be selling yourself short and cheating him.' And Rick Hunter slammed his door.

My blood, hot and fiery, raced through my body. My muscles tensed and my mind tossed his words over and over. Though why I was even listening to his opinion was beyond comprehension. The jerk. I was just dressing nicely.

The thought of introducing a guy to my pets first was ludicrous. As if a few harmless little pets were going to affect a relationship…

I stared out of my apartment window, coffee in my hand. I wanted so much to talk to someone about Rick-the preacher-Hunter, but my girlfriends wouldn't understand, being married. I needed someone single, someone who knew about being alone, knew about putting up with people—*and* knew about looking for love.

Courtney Jenkins waved to me from her apartment across the lane. I waved back.

I straightened tall and shot her a big smile. Bingo!

CHAPTER SIX

I STOOD on Courtney's doorstep, staring at her door, wondering if I was doing the right thing. But then, heck, what could she say? Nothing was worse than putting up with Rick Hunter and having no one to understand. I knocked.

The door opened.

'Hi, this sounds silly, but—'

'Come in, come in. We're neighbours, after all.' Courtney grabbed me by the arm and dragged me into her place. 'I'm so glad you came over.'

I smiled at her. She was gorgeous up close. Tall, blonde and willowy, with clear skin and green eyes. She wore a pair of blue trousers and a white shirt, as opposed to my black first-date dress.

Her apartment was to die for. What looked neat and clean from my window was actually pure luxury. The walls were pristine pastels, in lemon and white, the furniture cream and plush, the décor as though a decorator had been through and added all the little touches that make a room into a magazine spread.

I hesitated. She was so out of my league.

Courtney pushed me to the kitchen bench in the open-plan living area. She settled me onto a bar stool at her kitchen counter and fussed over making me a chocolate sundae—she knew me so well! My throat ached and my eyes stung. 'I came to ask your advice.'

'Has it got anything to do with that drop-dead gorgeous guy you're sharing your apartment with?'

'You're psychic?'

'Observant. Tell me, what's his name? He looks sort of familiar, but it's hard to tell at this distance.'

'Rick Hunter.'

Courtney shook her head slowly. 'No.' She shrugged. 'Oh, well, tell me everything.'

And I told her everything. Including how attracted I was to the very married man who was sharing my place with me. 'And I don't even know what sort of book he's writing,' I blurted. As if *that* was the drama!

Courtney leant against the bench and nibbled on her triple-choc biscuit. 'I don't know what to say. I haven't seen much of him. He keeps the curtains drawn most of the day and his light off, and the curtains open at night.'

'He likes the dark,' I said vaguely, my mind flooding with images of that first night when I'd pegged him for a burglar, and how he'd smelt so wonderful, had felt so divine…

'Maybe I should ask my ex if he could check him out for you. He's a cop.'

'That must be handy.' I looked around the up-market apartment. He must have been out of her league too.

'I'm an interior decorator,' Courtney said, obviously reading my expression. 'It's handy now, having him be a cop, but it wasn't when I was married to him. He was way too protective of James and I. Always going overboard in making sure I was safe. It's a wonder I'm not neurotic.'

'And now?' I know, not very tactful, but that's me—curiosity incarnate.

'Now he's tempered his fanatic attention.' Courtney sipped her tea. 'The distance helps him see us as more capable of looking after ourselves.'

I scooped another spoonful of ice cream in my mouth, feeling better about my life. Just sharing my woes with someone who understood was a relief, and of course it helped that she'd seen Rick and knew what I was up against. Knowing she was here to lean on again, if I needed her, was even better. I only hoped I could return the favour.

'I think it's strange his wife would let him board with a single woman. I'd avoid him until you meet his wife.'

'What happens if she doesn't come?'

'If I were in your situation…' her eyes went starry '…I'd be forcing the point. Get her there.

Get her to realise the situation he's in and let them battle it out. It's not fair he's torturing you like this. And I'd get on to your landlord too.'

'But what about my babies?' I whispered, my chest tight with the knowledge that she was right. It was time I seriously got rid of the guy.

'Just get some more background on your Rick Hunter. See if Al will give up some information on his cousin and his marriage. Maybe he'll even call the wife up and let her in on what's going on.'

I nodded, taking another scoop of the sundae. 'Great idea. Thanks.' I stared out of the window, feeling strange to be seeing what Courtney usually saw of me and my place.

I jerked to my feet.

Rick was standing squarely in the middle of my lounge room, staggering in circles, with Waldo my snake around his neck! 'I have to go. It looks like I've got a small domestic problem.'

Courtney strode to the window and stared across the way. She turned to me, her eyes wide. 'You go, girl. Or you may not have a Rick Hunter to worry about at all.'

I pushed my feet into my heels. 'I don't understand it. Waldo hasn't ever done anything like this before…'

Courtney opened her door and urged me on. 'Should I call an ambulance?'

'And say what? They'd think it was a joke! It may not be as bad as it looks.' I smirked, praying that was true. I also prayed that Rick Hunter wouldn't hurt Waldo, and I prayed that Waldo wouldn't hurt Rick. Why? I couldn't fathom. It wasn't as if I cared about the guy at all...

I burst in through my door, my heart hammering in my chest, my breath coming in ragged gasps. I really have to give up the ice cream. *Please let me not be too late.* I just wanted to get Rick Hunter out of my flat, not strangle him to death.

I dropped my keys as I ran into the lounge room to the body on the floor, my mind grappling to remember my first aid course. My veterinary training rushed to my mind—would it apply?

The body turned. 'He's under the sofa,' Rick said casually. He was fine, healthy, unharmed. He looked up at me with his bright eyes as though he was glad to see me.

I knew better. 'What the hell happened? You didn't hurt him, did you?' I knelt down beside the sofa, reaching out for Waldo. My hands were shaking. I yanked them back, praying Rick wouldn't see.

Rick sat up and stared me in the face, and shrugged. 'I was mucking around, that's all. Snakes aren't really that bad...but thanks for caring.'

My heart thudded into my ribs; fire poured into my veins. How dared he? 'You scared me half to death.'

He shot me a look and I got the distinct impression that was the point. Though why, I couldn't fathom. Why would he have a problem with me being at Courtney's? Or was it just that he'd missed me?

I shook my head, trying to clear my thoughts. 'What were you doing with him in the first place? He lives in the pantry.' I picked Waldo up carefully and took him back there. I placed him on the top shelf, stroking his cool, smooth skin.

'What were you doing over there?'

'You noticed?' Which substantiated the fact that he did look over there—a lot. The pang in my chest was both uncomfortable and alien to me.

'Well?' His deep voice held a challenge.

'Well, what? I'm not about to tell you my business. Besides, if you were looking you'd have seen I was visiting Courtney Jenkins and had a very nice time, thank you.'

'Surely you have other friends you can talk to.'

'I happen to like Courtney and I'll see as much of her as I like.' I glared him in the eye. 'Unless you have a specific reason why you don't want me over there.'

'I was worried, that's all.' He shrugged.

'About what, for goodness' sakes? Me?' I held my breath. Was it possible that Rick Hunter had a soft spot for me? My body warmed at the thought.

'She's not like you. She has a kid.'

I stiffened. Low blow. So it wasn't me. It was Courtney being corrupted by the likes of me! 'I did notice she has a child.' The ache in the back of my throat made the words come out funny. I avoided Rick's eyes as I brushed past him.

'I'm sorry. That came out wrong.' He caught my arm and it was as though his anger melted into something more disturbing. 'I've never met anyone as distracting as you.'

I was distracting? I swallowed hard, lifted my chin, and boldly met his gaze. 'From your book?' I offered. I didn't want to contemplate anything else. 'I'm distracting you from your book?'

There was a long pause. 'Yes,' he finally said, his eyes lowered, his branding grip loosening on my arm. 'From the book.'

'Good. I mean, that's bad. I mean—' I looked up into his eyes. Big mistake. They glowed with a savage fire that called to my body, firing my blood, awakening desires that I'd have rather stayed dormant.

He was pulling me closer to him.

I lifted my hands to his chest to push away. 'This isn't a good idea, Rick.'

'It feels good.' His other hand encircled my waist while his eyes burned into mine, daring me to deny what was between us.

I swallowed, a thousand excuses poised on my tongue. But only one really mattered. I opened my mouth, but my throat had gone tight. My whole body felt paralysed. There was something extremely mesmerising about Rick Hunter's mouth, and the way it was coming towards mine.

'I was thinking—' I blurted.

'This isn't the time for thinking.' Rick's hand slid up my back, urging me closer still. The pull in the pit of my stomach was like a magnetic attraction, an addiction, dangerous.

I struggled with myself, with the shivery sensations he was evoking throughout my body. It was an enormous effort to concentrate. 'You're married,' I choked out. 'Happily married.'

Rick stiffened. He stared down into my face. It was as though he wanted to tell me something. Something important.

'You did swear an oath to be faithful and dutiful, didn't you?' There was no way I could stomach ever being the 'other woman' again. Ever. Once had been enough for a lifetime and I'd learnt my lesson the hard way.

I had to get Rick to wake up to the beautiful gift of marriage, of having someone to love you, of never being alone, even if I was totally and utterly in love with the guy—which I definitely was not. 'Haven't you got a duty to your partner?' I pushed.

He dropped his hands and stepped back as if I'd scalded him, his eyes wide and his face grim.

I dragged in a breath, fighting the sting behind my eyes. I shouldn't have to put up with this. I strode to my bedroom and closed the door firmly. The sooner I got Mrs Hunter here, the better. She'd sort out her hubby and drive home his marital responsibilities.

I coughed away the ache in the back of my throat. I couldn't wait to be rid of him.

CHAPTER SEVEN

WORK was my sanctuary now, and I couldn't wait to get there. It was great. It was fulfilling. I loved my job—helping fix up animals that people brought in. And they came in all sizes, from fish and lizards to dogs the size of small ponies. And I had a great relationship with the vet. I loved the work and loved the animals.

I rolled out of bed, trying to not think about anything. I'd thought half the night, between fits of sleep—of my life, of the annoying Rick Hunter, and of my ex-boyfriends. Especially Alex.

Alex had been smooth. I should have known from the start, but instinct always goes astray when I'm dating. I don't know why. You'd think that would be the one time where my woman's intuition would work. But, no, my preservation instincts all go out of the window when the tall, dark and handsomes walk in the door.

Alex had oozed sex appeal. He'd taken me to all the nicest spots, wined and dined me into the bedroom, then broken my heart. Coming home early to find him in bed with another woman had been bad enough—but to be interrupted minutes into my tirade by his wife walking in the door and confronting us all...

Anger stirred again. Anger at the past, for being conned by such a lying jerk, and anger at Rick Hunter for his indiscretion. And anger at myself for just standing there like an idiot, begging to be kissed.

At least my room was tidy. I'd spent hours last night after leaving Rick tidying up my mess—I'd needed to do something with the pent-up energy he'd evoked. And my room looked great now. I went straight to my drawers and then grabbed a grey trouser suit from my cupboard.

I paused at my door. I didn't want to face Rick.

I lifted my chin and flung the door open. I was strong. I was fine. I was going to get his wife here and get rid of him.

'Good morning, Casey.'

I froze. Rick was on the floor. He wore a blue windcheater that made his chest look even wider, and those damn jeans. I stared at where his hands were rubbing George's tummy, my body aching.

George was in ecstasy, thumping his tail around wildly. Traitor.

'Rick,' I greeted him shortly, quelling my body's response. I couldn't wish him a good morning. I didn't want to wish him anything except a get-out-of-my-life. 'Oh, I wanted to ask you— what is your wife's name?'

'Why?' His eyes stabbed me as though I'd just demanded to know a national secret.

'One of the animals at work has just had babies and we need more names.' I looked at him expectantly, hoping he couldn't see the lie on my face. I thought I'd sounded quite convincing myself...

Rick looked at George. 'Ah...her name's... Stacey.'

'Great name. Thanks.' I escaped into the bathroom before Rick could distract me from my mission. There was nothing more important. I had to get rid of the guy as soon as I could. He was driving me crazy. He was getting too friendly. He was forgetting he was married.

Hot water only lasts so long, so I dried off and dressed for work, right then and there. There was no way I was walking around the apartment in just my dressing gown again. No way. I'd felt practically naked yesterday when Rick had waylaid me in his room. And the way his eyes had run over me... I shivered.

I smoothed down my suit, dragged long, slow breaths into my lungs, and willed myself to stay calm, cool and controlled. I could do this. I had her name. It was going to be easy.

I yanked open the door and strode across the room, noting Rick was by the window, staring out again. He turned.

'How's your book going?' I asked casually, keeping my feet moving, my voice even and my eyes averted.

A pause. 'Fine.'

I kept my focus on my bedroom door, scooping up the cordless phone as I went. 'Nearly finished?' It was wishful thinking. I'm sure it takes longer than a couple of days to write a book.

'Ah…no.'

I closed my door. Made it. So far, so pretty damned good. I dialled Enquiries to get a number for the noticeably absent Mrs Hunter. Nothing. I tried all combinations, but there were no Stacey Hunters in the greater Brisbane area.

Damn it. It was meant to be easy.

I glanced at my watch. There wasn't time now to find his wife. I had a full day at the clinic—the vet was booked out for appointments this morning, and there were two tumour operations and a castration to do in the afternoon.

With my purse slung over my shoulder, my shoes in my hand and the phone under my arm, I flung my door wide and strode into the kitchen. I dropped the phone on the bench, plucked a banana from the fruit bowl and headed for the door.

'Do you want to have dinner with me tonight?'

Rick's words stopped me mid-step. I turned slowly, trying to work out whether I'd heard him right or was having an aberration. 'Pardon?'

Rick sat on a chair by the window, George at his feet. 'Would you like to have dinner with me tonight?'

'I have a date. You know that,' I accused. 'Why don't you invite your wife? Is she up in Brisbane, or here in Melbourne?' I impressed myself with my subtlety in sliding in the question of his mystery wife's whereabouts.

'Brisbane?' Rick asked vaguely.

'You said you were from Brisbane.' Where else would he get his beautiful tan and keep his beautiful wife?

'Yes, of course—that's what I said.' Rick stood up and crossed his arms over his chest. 'No, we moved down six months ago. *My wife* and I. *Me* and her. Together.'

I stared at the guy. That explained my failure at finding a number for her. 'You did? Why? It's so lovely up there.'

Rick paused, staring at me as though I was a professor who had just asked him a tough question. 'For work,' he said finally.

'And what do you do when you're not trying to write a book?' Which was a good question I should have asked him at the start, but hadn't thought to. 'Are you on holiday or something?'

'Yes.' He stared down at George, who was unashamedly baring his belly for more rubbing. 'I'm on a break…to write my…book.' He didn't sound so sure.

'So, is your wife coming for dinner tonight?' I crossed my fingers. My salvation might all come at once. Meeting Mr Anthony Calahan, conservative and available accountant, possibly the man of my dreams, and getting rid of Rick in one fell swoop.

Rick nodded slowly, flashing his deep, dark blue eyes at me. 'Will you and your date stay here and have dinner if…my wife…comes?'

I bit my lip. I would have preferred to get to know Anthony Calahan privately, but then, curiosity was such a weight to bear. I ached to meet Rick Hunter's wife. It would do my sanity a great service to finally put a face to the image I had of her. 'I think that would be lovely. As long as my date doesn't mind.'

He glanced out of the window. 'Great. I'll cook something special. Can you pick up a nice bottle of wine?'

'Sure. Red or white?'

'White.'

'No problem,' I shot back, grabbing the necessities from my other purse on the hall stand. 'See you later.' And I left, with a weird sensation coursing through me. Was I actually becoming friendly with Rick Hunter, or was I falling into a trap?

* * *

I was stark, raving mad! I had to be. I was hurrying home to get ready for a blind date with one man, dinner with an irritatingly handsome guy who had been driving me crazy, *and* what could only be his drop-dead gorgeous wife. As if meeting Anthony wasn't going to be enough!

I gripped the bottle of wine tightly. The reality was intimidating—okay, terrifying—and I wondered how I could be such a victim to my curiosity.

I'd called Sophie as soon as I'd arrived at work, in between assisting the vet with tending a rabbit with a broken leg and a cat that had a chicken bone lodged in its mouth. Sophie had called her hubby, who'd called Anthony and conveyed the change of plan to everyone's satisfaction except mine. What was I doing? I didn't want to get to know a complete stranger with Rick Hunter's probing eyes on me.

I shook myself. He wouldn't be staring at me if his wife was there. And all the better if he did stare in front of her—show her the lie of the land she ought to be excavating her hubby from.

George greeted me at the front door. I bent down and ruffled his fur, then gave him a big hug. I was getting what I wanted, but could I cope with what I was about to get?

I dropped my keys on the hall stand, breathing in the spicy scents wafting my way. It smelt really wonderful.

'You're home—great.' Rick stood in the kitchen, his blue jeans covered with a multi-stained once-white apron, his black shirt showing off his muscular chest. 'Did you get the wine?'

'Yes,' I said vaguely, weathering the storm of sensation raging through my frustrated, tortured body. He even looked good when he wasn't try-ing—which made it all the more irritating.

'How was your day?'

'It was okay,' I answered easily. 'How about you? The book going well?'

There was a pause. 'Yes. The book is great.' He shot me a smile. 'Really getting some good ma-terial…things are great.' He wiped the bench, then looked up at me again. 'There is just this one spot I'm having…difficulty with. And I wanted to know if you…where's your family?'

'My family? You'd like to know about my fam-ily for your book?' Warmth stupidly filled my chest. It wasn't as if he *really* was interested about my family, about *me*. 'My father was a liar.'

Rick swallowed. 'A liar?'

'Yes, a liar.' I shrugged, kicking off my shoes. 'He kept telling Mum he'd given up drinking. He kept telling Mum he'd get a job. And he promised me our little family would always be together.'

'What happened?'

I placed the wine in the fridge to cool. 'I was eating cornflakes one morning—my ninth birthday, actually—and he told me he was popping out for cigarettes. He didn't come back.'

If Mum and he had actually married, he might have felt some obligation, some duty, some responsibility to come back...

'And your mother?'

I closed the fridge door and leant against it, watching Rick cleaning. He kept his back to me, which I appreciated. It was far easier talking to him when his dark, probing eyes weren't on me. 'She struggled for years to make ends meet, and then she got sick of struggling. She passed away four years ago.'

'I'm sorry.'

'What about you? Are your parents around?' I couldn't lose this opportunity or let my curiosity down. Finding out more about Rick Hunter was my mission.

Rick nodded. 'Yes, they're around.' He shrugged and turned. 'I had a happy childhood.'

I shot him a bolstering smile. I didn't want him feeling bad on my account for having the childhood I'd so desperately wanted for myself. 'So they do exist, then?'

'Yes, happy childhoods do.'

And he looked at me wistfully, as though he wanted to wrap me in his arms. Yeah, right. I was delusional. And the evening hadn't even begun!

Rick looked at his feet. 'I've got everything under control here, if you want to get ready.' He offered me a smile of encouragement.

I shot him a grin. 'Thanks.' I froze. What was this? Was I actually being friends with Rick? Why had I just told him the most intimate details of my past? I didn't want to be his friend. I wanted him gone. *Didn't I?*

CHAPTER EIGHT

I SLIPPED on a pair of black velvet trousers and a white lace shift, and my low-heeled white dress shoes. I pinned my hair up, put black pearl drops at my ears and stared dolefully at myself in the mirror. I was going to meet Rick's wife. I should be excited and relieved. But all I felt was a squeezing tightness in my chest and a deep ache in my belly.

The knock jerked me from my mood.

I strode to the front door. I had to be brave. I had to be strong. I had to get there before Rick, for some reason. Was his wife going to be tall and blonde? I swallowed hard. Or a brunette of average height and looks?

Rick was still in the kitchen, creating scents that enticed the senses—rich, heady and exotic. I couldn't miss the fact that he'd changed his clothes, though. He wasn't in his casuals any more—he was as smart as…

I faltered. Stopped.

Black trousers covered his long legs and a soft blue shirt with a turquoise silk tie framed his torso to suave perfection. His hair was neat, his face

247

clean-shaven, and his eyes were flashing as they roved over me with uncomfortable thoroughness.

My cheeks flushed under the heat of his gaze, my heart hammering against my ribs, every nerve yearning for his touch, his kiss, him.

The knock sounded again.

Please let it be his wife. Please. I backed away from Rick's intensity. 'I'll get it,' I croaked, lifting my finger and pointing somewhere in the vicinity of the door.

'You look beautiful,' he murmured, almost under his breath, except that I heard it, loud and clear.

I turned, fled to the door and flung it wide. It wasn't his wife.

'Hello, sorry I'm late.' The man's eyes slid down my body and up again. 'I'm Anthony Calahan.'

'Casey,' I offered, holding out my hand. Anthony had sandy hair, hazel eyes and a round face. He was as tall as Rick was, although of a lighter frame, or was that just because he pushed a pencil rather than…? What? I still had no idea what Rick did for work. I caught myself. Why was I comparing him to Rick anyway?

Anthony wrapped my hand in his thin, long one. 'Absolutely lovely to meet you.' His voice was thin and nasal.

I managed a smile. Why didn't I listen to myself about blind dates? About picking strangers up from cafés—from anywhere? I sucked in a deep, slow breath. I was being silly. It wasn't as though I'd know at first sight that he was wrong for me. He could be a lovely person, perfectly suited to me—my soul mate, a kindred spirit.

'Come in,' Rick called, his voice deep and velvet-smooth. 'Or you'll let the animals out.'

I stiffened. What was that? Was Rick planning on introducing this guy to my pets? Was this all a set-up so he could prove his theories?

'Maybe we should go out somewhere?' I whispered to my date.

Anthony dragged in a deep breath. 'Smells wonderful. You've gone to so much trouble. I wouldn't hear of it.'

I stepped back and let my so-blind date in. Who cared anyway? As long as Rick's wife turned up and I got Rick turned out…nothing else mattered. Or did it?

I wanted that house with the picket fence. I wanted a family to call my own. Was that so wrong?

Rick strode right up to Anthony. 'Rick Hunter. Great to meet you.' And he shot me a look—of challenge, or triumph?

'Anthony Calahan.' They shook hands vigorously.

'Come in, sit down, make yourself at home. Would you like a glass of wine?' Rick offered, playing the perfect host despite the fact it was my place, not his, and my night, not his.

'Love one, thank you.' Anthony headed for the lounge. I stopped and redirected him. Why sit down there when we could settle at the table and get this night on the way to being over?

I pulled out a chair for him, next to me, staring at the four settings. There was no way I was going to avoid Rick tonight. He'd either be sitting next to me or opposite me. First thing tomorrow I'd get a bigger table!

'Casey, could you get the wine? I have to get back to the meal.' And Rick walked back to the kitchen, leaving me with Anthony and the most awkward silence I'd been in for a while. I didn't know whether to start explaining the arrangement or just run.

Anthony looked up at me. 'Is his date running late?'

'We're waiting on his wife, actually.' I sucked in a deep breath. 'I'll just grab your drink.' I spun around and dashed to the kitchen. 'What are you doing?' I whispered harshly to Rick.

Rick lifted the lid off a bubbling curry, raising an eyebrow as though he was innocent. 'Cooking.'

'You know what I mean. Why did you say that about my pets getting out? To let him know I had animals?' I whispered. 'Congratulations. But he didn't run out screaming, did he?'

Rick moved close to me. 'The night is young,' he said quietly. Then he had the nerve to give me a smile. I could have punched him. The only saving factor was that his wife was coming and she might be none too impressed at her hubby having a black eye—and me nursing broken knuckles…

I poured a glass of wine for Anthony and one for myself. 'Do *you* want one?'

'I'll have whatever you're offering.' Rick kept his eyes on the stove, but a devilish grin pulled at his sensuous mouth.

My grip tightened on the bottle. I knew he was teasing but I couldn't help but react—all over. '*Would* you like a glass of wine?' I asked, carefully, calmly and as coolly as I could manage while my blood raced hot and fiery through my body. How dared he play with me?

'Love one. Thank you, Casey.' He flicked off the stove and tipped the contents of the pots into serving dishes.

A shiver ran down my spine at my name on his lips. I concentrated on the food instead.

One of the dishes contained exotic saffron rice. Another dish contained a curry, steaming hot and spicy, cleaning my nasal passages so efficiently I knew I'd approach that one carefully. Another held a vegetable dish with what looked like eggplant, tomato, potato, pumpkin and carrots. A platter held some fried Indian bread, all golden brown and puffed like flaky footballs.

My mouth watered at the sight, at the scent, and at the idea I was going to be sitting down and partaking in this feast within minutes. 'Where on earth did you learn to cook all this?'

'I get around,' he shot back, lifting two of the serving dishes—mismatched, because I never seem to collect enough tokens to get the whole set of anything.

'Are you a cook?' I asked.

'No, I just enjoy it. You use a recipe, follow the instructions to the letter, and *voilà*, you have a meal.' He flashed me a boyish grin as though I'd patted him on the back for a mud-pie well made.

My heart fluttered. I'd found the boy in the man. He *loved* to cook. Really, truly loved it. My entire body warmed and I blinked away the sting in my eyes. I'd seen something few would know about the tough-looking guy in front of me. Except maybe his wife…

'Where's your wife?' I blurted, glancing at my watch, pushing down the sensations causing havoc with my goal. It was well past eight. 'What time did she say she was going to be here?'

'She…said seven.' He shrugged and made his way to the table. 'So Anthony, what do you do for work?'

I picked up the remaining two dishes and followed. There was no way I was going to sit idly by and wait for his wife to turn up—every minute that passed built the coiled anticipation inside my belly.

Anthony turned to face Rick. 'I'm an accountant at a firm in Toorak. Been there for a few years now. What do you do?'

'Don't you think you should call her?' I urged, a pace behind Rick. 'She could be lost—'

'She'd call if she were lost. Is your family local, Anthony?' Rick placed his load on the table and started serving the rice and curries onto plates with the dexterity of a seasoned waiter.

Anthony flicked his napkin across his lap—where had Rick found *them*? 'Yes. Melbourne born and bred. The folks are out at Eltham.'

I leant on the back of my chair, gripping it tightly. I didn't care about what Anthony did, or where he grew up, or where his parents lived—I just wanted to know where Rick's wife was. 'Don't you think you ought to find out if she's okay?'

Rick laid the serving spoon down and pulled out his chair. 'Let's eat. If she isn't here by dessert I'll send out a search party, okay?' He offered me a smile, then sat down as though he hadn't a concern in the world.

The seat Rick chose, facing Courtney's place, didn't escape my notice. Nor did the way he'd consistently avoided Anthony's questions. Or the way he was looking directly at me.

I concentrated on the meal, which was absolutely the best thing I'd ever tasted—and I've had a lot of take-out in my life—trying not to think about Rick looking at me, or about his absent wife. And I have to say I wasn't doing a good job of ignoring him at all.

CHAPTER NINE

ANTHONY and Rick dominated the conversation—though I was contributing up until they started on sports. My mind wandered back to the missing wife and why in hell Rick wasn't concerned about her. Didn't he love her? A traitorous warmth crept into my chest and down into my belly.

Rick stood up, gathering the dirty dishes.

I stood up too.

'You stay. I'll get the coffee,' Rick offered.

'I'll help.' I shot him a look of pure murder. It was nine-thirty and there wasn't a sign or a squeak from Mrs Stacey Hunter. I followed him into the kitchen and dumped the dishes on the sink.

'She's not coming, is she?' I whispered harshly at him, a sense of icy foreboding seeping into my pores.

'No.'

'Thank you for being so honest,' I bit out sarcastically, glaring at the guy as though I wanted to nail him to the wall. 'Did you even invite her?'

'Not exactly.' And he stared out of the window to Courtney's place as though I was just so easy to ignore.

My mind jerked. My blood chilled. Was Courtney his wife? It was a crazy thought, but his preoccupation with the view couldn't be ignored. I looked out too. Courtney was washing dishes at her sink. 'She looks so alone, doesn't she? Maybe we should invite her over for coffee.'

'No.' The word burst from Rick's mouth. He crossed his arms over his chest. 'No,' he managed, more calmly. He dropped his arms and pushed his hands into his pockets. 'You wouldn't want her to come over and interrupt your night with Anthony.'

I crossed my arms over my chest, giving Rick my best rendition of the evil eye. 'Really? And what exactly have you been doing all night, then?'

'Being polite.' Rick pulled at his tie, loosening it and slipping it from his neck. 'And cooking. Put the kettle on, will you?' And he strode towards his room. 'Anthony, how about you sit in the lounge area and we'll bring over some coffee?' he said loudly.

Anthony scraped his chair across my polished timber floorboards. 'Sounds great.'

Rick opened the door to his room and George bounded out straight to Anthony, to check him out. He leapt around at his feet in the wild frenzy that only small dogs with big appetites for affection seem to affect.

Anthony put up his hands to ward George off, but my baby doesn't know rejection. He leapt up beside my guest and snuggled into him for a cuddle.

I wasn't blind. I wasn't stupid. I could see instantly that Anthony wasn't a hands-on, pets sort of guy. And I could see the smirk of satisfaction plainly on Rick's arrogant face!

'I thought he was in *my* room,' I shot at Rick, giving him a glare worthy of Medusa herself. I could see exactly what he was doing and I was not impressed. So he wanted to prove his point? I'd show him where to shove his point.

Rick tossed his tie into his room, wandered back to the lounge and dropped his tall frame into a chair, looking pretty damned pleased with himself. 'He wanted to go in my room.'

'Really?' I gritted my teeth, fighting the urge to fly across the room and knock the wind out of Rick Hunter with my fists—or the frying pan.

Rick leant back in the chair and crossed his arms over his head. 'Is that kettle on?'

I snatched up the kettle, filled it with water and flicked the damned thing on. If he thought I was going to sit helplessly by while he ruined my date, he had another think coming!

'Your dog?' Anthony asked Rick.

'No, Casey's. Isn't he the most friendly fur-ball this side of the Westgate Bridge?' And he shot me a smile that shone pure mischief in his eyes.

I wished he hadn't tidied the bench…I could so easily have thrown something at him! But all there was were the pots, far too heavy for me to hurl and make the distance and the stirring spoons, too light to make an impression in his head if I managed to hit him.

Anthony rubbed George's head tentatively. 'Nice dog.'

I stuck out my tongue at Rick. He ignored me, casting a long glance out of the window. Again. My belly clenched tight. There had to be something up with Courtney and him. Had to be. And, curiosity being my curse, I would just have to find out what…

I dived into the cupboard in search of three matching mugs. I emerged triumphant—and none of them were even chipped—after only a few minutes. There was some good in having Rick around cleaning everything all the time—it would have taken me hours to find matching mugs before he came along.

Rick sat back on his lounge chair, a smile on his face as though he was the fox who'd just swallowed a hen and got away with it.

The sofa was empty. 'Where's Anthony?'

'I suggested he might like to use the bathroom. You know—wash his hands…'

My legs moved of their own volition.

I was facing Rick Hunter in a millisecond.

He got up out of the chair and looked down at me. 'Got a problem, Casey? Are you scared that your new boyfriend isn't going to like Caesar?'

I opened my mouth but no words came out. I was inches from Rick Hunter's gorgeous body, his deep dark eyes and his taunting mouth. And Anthony was going to meet my turtle. But all I could think of was how nice Rick smelled, all male and spicy, and that Rick had remembered Caesar's name. My skin prickled.

The bathroom door swung open. Anthony walked out, his brow creased. 'You know you have a turtle in the sink?'

'In the *sink*?' I shot Rick a look of pure disgust. How dared he push this pet thing? If I hadn't known he was so perfectly, happily married—to a very absent wife—I'd have thought he was jealous.

I stalked into the bathroom, plucked Caesar out of the sink and put him back in the bath. I had a couple of inches of water in the deep end and a rocky terrain at the other, behind the shower curtain.

I heard the door slam.

I lurched out of the bathroom. What had Rick done now?

Rick lounged in the chair, where I'd left him. Anthony was nowhere in sight. 'Where is he?' I demanded, throwing my chest out and placing my hands on my hips—rather than around his throat. I'd had about enough meddling from Rick Hunter for one night!

'Gone. He had to go.' Rick rose from his chair and sauntered to the kitchen.

'Why?' I whispered, my mind grappling with Anthony's unexpected exit. 'Where?'

Rick shrugged, picked up a sponge and started wiping down the stove. 'It wasn't as if he was going to suit you. He wasn't your type.'

'And you know *my type*?' I challenged, my blood heating, my legs feeling suspiciously like jelly. How could such a perfect night—in theory— go so darned wrong? 'And what type is that, exactly?'

Rick lifted his hands, warding me off. 'Do you want that coffee? You look like you could do with a coffee. Or do you want something stronger?'

I slumped into the cushions of the sofa. I'd got nothing at all. No new boyfriend and no wife to drag Rick Hunter out of my life. And no idea why Anthony had left in such a hurry. Was there something seriously wrong with having pets?

I felt movement behind me. I slipped my hand under the cushions and felt Waldo's cool body, slithering into a more comfortable position—*on my sofa*! I swung to face Rick. 'You…you—' Hot, clawing anger poured through my veins. How dared he? How could he?

There was no way was I going to let Anthony Calahan, conservative accountant, walk out of my life without an explanation. Or let Rick Hunter manipulate my life, no matter what his stupid motives. Though I would be very interested to hear them.

I jerked to my feet and strode to the door.

'What are you doing?' Rick asked.

I didn't even look at him. I couldn't. Nothing was going to stop me, least of all Rick's deep blue eyes and velvet-soft voice. 'None of your damned business.'

I slammed the door after me, giving myself a bolstering swell of satisfaction. If Rick hadn't guessed already how close I was to murdering him, he'd have an idea now.

Anthony stood on the landing, shifting on his feet, staring at the panel above the lift indicating which floor it was on. Thank God for the fickle lift. 'Anthony, wait.'

He turned towards me and the look on his face said it all. I faltered. It wasn't a look of uninterest; it was fear.

'I'm sorry, Casey, but I can't—' He coughed, looked down at his feet, then up at the panel again.

'He's a very docile python. He's not as danger-ous as he looks.'

I would have worked out that he was afraid of snakes before we married—he probably wouldn't have discovered my python in the pantry until well after our anniversary. Second or third, at least!

He blinked several times. 'That may be, but—'

'It's an awful lot to take on in one night,' I argued, the growing realisation dawning on me that unless I convinced Anthony I was worth an-other date I'd be back to square one—all alone with Rick Hunter again. 'But pythons aren't dangerous. They're really no big deal.'

'Casey…' he said softly.

This was it. This was when he'd ask me out again. That would show Rick. I sucked in my breath and waited, widening my eyes in that vulnerable, maiden-in-distress sort of way I'd been practising in the mirror.

'What's your relationship with Rick Hunter?'

I stepped back, expelling the air from my lungs in a rush. 'He's a boarder, that's all.' Anthony shot me a look that I couldn't quite discern—as if he didn't believe me. 'His wife *was* coming, you know,' I lied, crossing my arms over my chest.

The lift dinged its arrival. And Anthony Calahan, my little house in the suburbs with the white picket fence and my saviour from Rick Hunter, was gone.

I paced the hall in front of my door, my mind a mass of tangled thoughts, my body a mass of tortured nerves. What was I doing to myself? It wasn't as though this was the only date I was ever going to get. It wasn't as though I was going to have to put up with Rick and his irritating ways for long… It wasn't as though I even cared!

He wasn't going to get the best of me. I hadn't spent seventeen months as a committed celibate to have him walk through my door and ruin all my hard-won realisations.

I racked my mind for which realisations exactly I was thinking about. I shook my head. That wasn't the issue. He wasn't going to get away with this, no matter what!

The door swung wide, whacking the wall with a satisfying thud—though Al would probably complain next inspection.

Rick was washing dishes in the kitchen. He looked up and met my blazing eyes—and froze.

I reduced the distance between us, my fists clenched firmly at my sides. I wasn't sure if I was going to use them—especially seeing as the last time I hadn't come out so well, and then I'd had the frying pan as well as my wussy, never-punched-anyone fists. 'How dare you?'

'What?' he asked innocently, wiping his hands on a towel. He tossed the cloth onto the bench casually and faced me as though nothing had happened at all.

I advanced on him. I wasn't going to buy the innocent act. I wasn't about to let him off. 'How dare you presume you can manipulate tonight to give Anthony a not-so-pleasant introduction to my pets?'

Rick cast a look to the sofa. 'Ah, you found Waldo.' And he looked to the door as though he was deducing my way of thinking when I'd rushed out.

'Yes, I found Waldo,' I growled. 'And I'm guessing Anthony did too, which would explain his very hasty exit.'

But Rick didn't look sheepish, guilty, or anything else except damned attractive. And he was staring at me as though there wasn't a wife on the planet.

He was right there, inches away from me, his cologne taunting me, his eyes intense, hot and promising. His look was galvanising, sending shivers racing up my spine.

A hot ache grew in my chest, clouding my mind, igniting my senses. Words eluded me.

He stepped closer still.

My heart thundered and it was all I could do to drag air into my lungs. My eyes were glued to his. And his were burning with promises.

He dropped his gaze to my lips.

My mind screamed danger. My body welcomed it.

Rick pulled me roughly to him, his hands branding the bare flesh of my shoulders. He lowered his head and his lips captured mine.

His mouth was warm, soft and gentle; his kiss was deep and plundering, awakening my body to a magic I'd never felt before in my life.

I ached for him, to taste more of him, have more of him, share everything with him. Heat consumed me and I kissed him back in complete abandon.

Rick's arms wrapped around me, encasing me in his warmth, holding me close against his hard body. And his lips savoured mine, lingering, tasting, delving.

I touched Rick, running my hands up his muscled chest, feeling his pounding heart beneath my fingertips.

A heart that was given to another.

I pulled back, wrenching myself out of his grasp. What had I done? I was so eager. My response so wanton. How could I have kissed Rick Hunter, a married man?

My hand jerked back, palm flat, and I swung, connecting with Rick's face with an objection he couldn't ignore.

'What the—?' Rick grabbed my wrist and stared down into my eyes, looking for all the world as if he was going to kiss me again.

My stomach fluttered. I shook myself. This was so wrong. 'You're married, remember?' I almost choked on the words.

He closed his eyes, paused, then opened them. 'Casey,' Rick whispered, his tone soft, his eyes beseeching, 'I want to talk to you about—'

I looked away. I knew what was coming, and I'd heard my fair share of lies. 'I don't want to talk to you at all—about your marriage, or that she's going to divorce you, or that you're actually separated, or that you're staying together because of the kids.'

He stepped back as though my words were punches. 'You've been lied to a fair bit, I take it?'

'Damn right I have. And I'm never, ever falling for a liar again!' I crossed my arms across my chest and lifted my chin to glare into his cheating face, ignoring my still-tingling lips. 'So, no matter what you say, I'm not going to listen.'

He stood and stared at me, his face grim, his brow furrowed, as though he was fighting with himself.

I didn't care. He could fight with his morals and his wife all he liked, I wasn't going to get involved! 'I think you can pack your bags.'

He sobered. 'I'm sorry.' He stepped further away from me and ran a hand through his hair. 'It won't happen again. I promise.'

'Damn right it won't.' I turned away, tears stinging my eyes. I knew what I had to do. I should have done it from the start. I should never have gone into this arrangement without an insurance policy. I knew more than anyone that all men were liars—married or not.

'Where are you going?' Concern laced his voice.

'Out.' I snatched my bag off the hall table and stormed through the door. It was well past time to turn the tables on Rick Hunter. And I knew just the way to do it.

CHAPTER TEN

I wasn't about to put up with any more nonsense from the chest-thumping he-man who had decided to share my apartment. No, slash that—the man who'd aided and abetted in blackmailing me into sharing my apartment with him!

My plan was to go to Sophie's place. I figured her husband would know how to find people. I'd go to her place and lay the whole mess on the table.

So, I'd already failed miserably in trying to find Mrs Hunter. So, she hadn't turned up for dinner. I wasn't about to give up on her when my comfort was on the line—and my sanity. I wouldn't be able to take Mr Hunter's deep, dark blue eyes for much longer. Or the rest of him.

I reached the foyer, my blood cooling a little, and stared at the front entrance mournfully. I wasn't in any hurry to admit to my friend that I'd corrupted a man from his matrimonial vows. Or that a married man was having such sport corrupting me.

I turned slowly on the spot, half tempted to crawl back upstairs, hide in my room and try to forget anything had happened tonight at all.

Al's door stood a metre away. Courtney's suggestion came to mind. He'd know about his cousin, and he'd know his cousin's wife—and her number. And if I was going to survive another night with Rick Hunter in my place I was going to have a few aces up my sleeve.

I didn't hesitate. Or think. I hammered on the timber.

Al groaned and muttered all the way to his door. I could hear the TV blaring, but I could hear his curses better. He flung open the door. 'What?'

'I need to speak to you about your cousin—Rick Hunter,' I blurted, praying my brain would come up with some brilliant way to broach the subject without sounding like a twit.

Al put his hands on his hips, making his belly seem even larger than it was. 'Really? What has he done now?'

'I can't say, exactly,' I faltered. There was no way I was going to say that he'd kissed me. The last thing I wanted was Al gossiping all over the building that I'd corrupted a married man.

'What do you want from me?' he snapped, scratching his chest like an oversized baboon. 'We have a deal.'

I dragged in a deep breath and let loose. 'I would like to know more about him, if you don't mind. I don't like sharing my place with a stranger.'

Al stared at me as though I was a bloodthirsty mosquito. 'Well, you're going to share with him—or you'll be winning yourself an eviction notice.'

I opened my mouth to say something brilliant. I swear, truly I was. But nothing came out.

'Albert, you're missing all the best parts.' The screech was unmistakably Mrs Blight, coming from the depths of their apartment.

'Look, you put up with…my cousin…and I'll put up with your dog and whatever else you've got in there.' And he slammed the door in my face.

I sat on the steps for a while, commiserating with myself. I'd got nowhere. No closer to finding out more about Stacey than before. I was half tempted to knock again, but I wasn't sure how to ask for Stacey Hunter's number without upsetting Al even more. And I didn't need him upset with me, for George's sake.

I trudged up the stairs. I would just have to find her another way. Old Albert was not going to be of any help. *Albert*. I can't remember ever thinking Al was for Albert.

I froze, my blood chilling. Rick didn't call him Albert at all. He called him Alan. That meant that either Al's wife had been drinking too much or Rick Hunter wasn't Al's cousin. And if he wasn't Al's cousin why on earth would Al be making me rent my room to him? I swallowed a lump in my throat. And why did Rick want it?

*   *   *

I managed to sneak out in the morning without encountering Rick Hunter. He'd probably planned it that way. He probably didn't want to speak to me either, reminding him of what he'd done last night. Or maybe he was scared I would go through with my threat and really throw him out! I wished I could, but George…

I stepped off the tram after work and smoothed out the creases in my trousers—from sitting down in one spot too long all day—and wrapped my pink cardigan tighter around my blouse. I hoped that he regretted his rash action as much as I regretted my response to him.

What was he going to tell his wife? I couldn't imagine the confession. *If there was going to be one*.

I walked slowly home. Work had been a refreshing relief from the intensity of my home life. I was in no hurry at all to race home and face the stranger in my place. I would have stayed at the clinic if the vet had let me.

I'd considered all sorts of possibilities all day—about who Rick was and why he'd want to stay in my place—and I'd come up with zip. Okay, so I had come up with all sorts of ideas, from spy plots to some angel's idea of teaching me a lesson. None seemed plausible.

My building seemed full of foreboding. Everything appeared the same, but I knew there was trouble waiting for me upstairs. And I knew because I was going to cause it.

I knew there wasn't much I could do about this turn of events except demand to know the truth from Rick himself. I had considered the possibility of going to the police at one point today, to inform them about Rick not being Al's cousin, but I dismissed it on the grounds that they'd laugh in my face.

Rick hadn't threatened anything except my sanity—and my lips. And I couldn't very well admit he was a party to blackmail without admitting that Al had played his part and I did, in fact, have George in my flat. I knew I just had to work this out myself.

I took the elevator up and stalked to my door, resolved to face the cute-looking, two-timing jerk inside and let him have it—have the whole verbal onslaught. And see what he'd do next. And what I would do.

The apartment was deathly quiet. 'George?' I called, staring around the place carefully. Nothing. I glanced at the hall stand, where I usually dumped George's leash. It was gone.

My chest warmed. Rick had taken George for a walk. For a jerk he certainly looked after my dog nicely. Maybe I was being too melodramatic. Maybe it was just a silly mistake that Rick had called his cousin the wrong name. Perhaps he'd never meant to kiss me...

Why wait to find out? I strode into Rick's room, my heart pounding. There was no reason I couldn't find out the truth myself. There had to be an answer in his room as to why he'd lied.

It looked the same as last time. The curtains were pulled closed, the bed-roll made neatly, all his paraphernalia set out in a line along the wall.

'What the hell are you doing?' Rick's voice stabbed into me with the proficiency of a missile.

I spun around. He wore tight blue denims and a white polo shirt, his jaw sporting a shadow, his eyes blazing. 'Trying to find out who you really are,' I snapped, quelling my body's response to him.

He stared. Speechless. 'You know who I am,' he said finally, crossing his arms over his chest.

I straightened. This was it. Was I going to skulk off to my room or face the guy? 'I know you're not Al's cousin.'

He hesitated. 'And why do you think that?' he said casually, as though we were talking about lunch and not lies.

'Because Al's name isn't Alan, it's Albert.' I had to smile at my brilliant detective work. I had Rick Hunter now.

'Oh.'

'Yes.' I nodded. I had won a point! And I was right. I frowned, recalling all the far-fetched motives I'd supposed he had. 'So, who in hell are you and why did you choose my place?'

Rick advanced on me, his face resolute, his movements determined, committed, scary.

I moved backwards, knocking into the dresser-cum-makeshift-desk. I caught a change of light and colour in the corner of my eye. The screensaver had flicked off on Rick's laptop.

I turned towards it. Courtney's apartment appeared—and so did Courtney, walking across her lounge.

I swung around, the pieces falling into place. 'She's your wife, isn't she? You're the husband who's the cop and over-protective.' It made sense. He was neat. Logical. Methodical. Stern. Commanding. Irritating. Handsome as hell.

My stomach clenched tight and my throat ached. I was sure I was right. I had to be. It was the only reasonable explanation I could think of. And it made me ill. This could only mean one thing. That he loved her with all his heart and wanted her back.

Rick reduced the distance between us. 'No.'

I didn't want him closer. I couldn't trust myself to have him closer—muddling my mind, causing havoc in my body. 'Stop.'

I swallowed hard, staring up into his dark and dangerous eyes. I had to be right. She had to be his ex. My chest ached and my eyes stung. Rick was lying. Again.

'Let me explain.'

'I don't want to hear it.'

'You don't understand.' Rick ran a hand through his hair and stared at the ceiling.

I took the opportunity to move. I swung the curtains wide—a small camera was set up in the corner. 'You don't have to explain anything. I do understand.' I didn't really. I was more confused than ever. What I wanted was to run and hide and cry away the tearing ache in the back of my throat.

'I don't have a wife.'

I turned and stared at him, the words sinking into my mind, a bubble of hope stirring deep in my chest. 'So you're just a plain liar, not a married one?'

'No,' Rick whispered softly, moving closer. 'And yes. Please, Casey…I can explain.'

He was a liar. The fact bounced around in my brain, knocking the memories of all the lies that had been fed to me in the past to the fore, making me dizzy. I felt small. I felt shattered. I felt ill.

Rick reached out for me.

I couldn't move. Or I just didn't want to. Maybe I wanted to pretend for one minute that it was all okay—that I could be his for one small moment in time. That I could have found someone just for me, meant for me, for a minute or two.

Rick touched my cheek and traced my jaw with his thumb, his eyes shining deep and blue and intense. 'Casey…' He brushed his thumb over my lips, sending shivers spiralling down my spine.

His lips brushed mine with a feather-light tenderness.

I closed my eyes and let the waves of sensation wash through me. It was a kiss a tired soul could melt into, drown in, get lost in. And I did. I parted my lips and his kiss deepened, arousing every nerve in my body to his spell. I leant into him.

He wrapped his arms around me, encasing me in his warmth, in his strength, in his life.

I ran my hands around his waist. He felt as hard and tough as he looked, but oh-so-warm. I moved my hands up his back, over the muscles rippling under my fingertips, up his neck, through his soft dark hair.

My entire being ached for him, for more, and it was all I could do to keep my hands where they were. I wanted to run my hands over his hot skin, taste him, share my body with him, give him my heart.

This was just for a moment. It could never be. Rick Hunter might not be married, but he was a liar. My eyes burned under my lids.

He might be the only guy I'd ever met who liked my pets. He might be the cleanest guy I'd ever met. He might be the only guy I'd ever met who made me feel…like this. But it didn't change the fact he was a liar. A manipulative liar who'd probably paid Al to blackmail me. *He was just like all the rest.* Unless he had a perfectly reasonable explanation…

Rick's hands cupped my face. He pulled back. 'You're crying.'

I swiped my cheeks and stiffened. 'Am not. It was just a bit of dust, that's all…' *Please, give me the perfectly reasonable explanation.*

'Casey.' He reached for me.

I shook my head, trying to swallow away the lump in my throat. 'No.' Not without an explanation.

I stared out of the window to Courtney's place… I couldn't help but sigh. She had so much, and now she had a date too. 'I'm glad,' I managed, though I was sure my skin was turning green with envy.

Rick frowned. 'What?'

I relaxed. I'd broken the mood, and I was more than keen to go on with the distraction. 'Courtney's getting lucky. She—'

Rick jerked around and strode to the window. 'She's not getting lucky. She's in trouble.'

I squinted at the guy who had his arms around Courtney's shoulders, who was pushing her onto the floor. It didn't look exactly like trouble to me… I ran my tongue over my lips. It looked very promising indeed…

Rick swung around. 'Damn it. I knew I should've picked another damned apartment. You're too damned distracting.' He cast the words over his shoulder as he raced out through the door.

I followed. Stupid, I know. But, curiosity being a curse I have to live with…

I had a hard job keeping up with Rick. He certainly was fit. But with a body like his it was no surprise he was in peak condition, leaving my chocolate-laden body a good minute or three behind.

He took the stairs in Courtney's building. I waited for the lift, panting, my mind a mass of questions. Like, if Rick thought she was in trouble, why didn't he just call the cops? Why had Rick been watching her anyway? *Was* he her fanatic ex? Had he just lied to me again?

My head was filled with jumbled thoughts; my body was a mass of traitorous tingling nerves that were more than willing to entice my mind into Rick's arms again.

I stepped out of the lift just as Rick kicked the door down—just like in the movies! I heard the splintering of wood as the door flew open, taking half its frame with it. The noise echoed so loudly down the hall I was sure all the neighbours would come out to see what drama was unfolding. They didn't. I raced forward as he plunged in.

Rick lunged at the guy who was manhandling Courtney on the floor. Her hair was ruffled, her halter-top askew. He hauled the guy off her and threw his weight onto him, sending them both crashing into the coffee table.

'Stop! What in—? *Stop!*' Courtney's voice was shrill.

Rick and the bloke on the floor froze, Rick's fist poised above the guy's face, ready to punch the guy into next week.

Courtney looked at me, bewildered. 'What are you doing here?'

'Saving you from this guy?' I guessed. Rick must really be the jealous type not to want his ex-wife to date anyone…

'This is my date.' She glared at Rick's back as though she wanted to do a bit of punching too. *'He's my date.'*

'Your *date*?' Rick collapsed onto his back on the floor. 'It looked like—' He covered his face with his hands as though he could wipe the last few minutes from existence.

'What, exactly—?' Courtney gave Rick a long, hard look. 'What, exactly, did you think?'

Rick dropped his hands and sat up, propping his elbows on his knees, appearing cool and calm, ready to face the music.

Courtney shook her finger at Rick, tilting her head. 'Hey, aren't you my ex-husband's partner? What are you doing here? Has Joe sent you to look out for me?' She stepped back. 'Tell me what's going on or I'm calling the police.'

Rick *wasn't* her ex? I expelled the breath in my lungs, a warmth of delicious proportions spreading through my body.

Courtney's date plucked himself off the floor and stood up, straightening his clothes.

My mind spun with the facts. I had no idea what it all meant! Rick was Courtney's ex's partner? He was a cop?

Rick jerked to his feet, stabbing me with a fierce glare. 'You're a darn distraction—you know that?' Rick turned to Courtney. 'Joe sent me to look out for you, okay. One of the crims he sent away got out. He was worried for you and James.'

'So you decided to stake out my apartment?' Courtney accused, her voice shrill.

'Yes.' Rick crossed his arms over his chest.

I shook my head, staring at my windows across the way. I was sorry for helping ruin her date. But I was also sick with jealousy that her ex-husband could still care for her so much that he'd send his mate to look after her.

I felt a swell of excitement in the pit of my belly. Rick wasn't Courtney's husband.

But he was some sort of cop, undercover, at my place, and lying to me. *Really* lying to me!

Ice seeped into my bones. My legs moved by themselves. Out of Courtney's place. Away. My throat ached with the pain of knowing I had nothing.

'Wait, Casey!'

Rick's voice was commanding, but I wasn't going to stop for anything. I already felt a complete idiot. I wasn't about to wait around for another instalment.

'Please, Casey.' He was following me.

I strode to the lift, paused, then turned. 'It was all lies, wasn't it? Everything?' I bit out, stifling the onslaught of emotion threatening to choke me. 'You're not an aspiring author.'

'No.'

I punched the button and stared at the lift doors, willing them to open in record time. 'You bribed Al to get yourself into my place, didn't you?'

'Yes.'

'You're not married?' I don't know why I asked—some warped, masochistic tendency to get any remnants of self-esteem firmly and thoroughly butchered.

'No.'

I gritted my teeth, stifling the hysterical laugh that threatened to erupt. All that pain, all that torture, all that recrimination when there was never a Mrs Hunter at all.

The lift doors opened and I stepped in, turned around and faced the stranger I'd shared my place with for the last few days. '*Is* your name Rick Hunter?'

'No.'

My eyes stung at the irony. Nothing was real at all. 'Then I have nothing else to say to you. You're a liar and a stranger to me.'

And the lift doors closed, blocking out the man, the liar, the stranger who had wormed his way under my skin and into my heart. *I should have known better.*

CHAPTER ELEVEN

GEORGE greeted me at the door with a yap of pleasure. I buried my face in his fur, soaking up the comfort. Then I jerked to my feet. I couldn't dither around. He could be back at any minute and there was no way I wanted to confront him again tonight. Or ever.

Rick whoever-he-was was a liar.

Rick whoever-he-was was a manipulative bastard, like every other guy that had come into my life.

I slammed my door and dropped onto the bed, my chest aching with a deep and solid pain. There was no use denying it. I was in love with Rick whoever-he-was. Totally and utterly. I slapped myself in the head. I'd done it again. Fallen for a guy only to have my heart smashed into little pieces.

I punched my pillows. I wasn't going to cry. I wasn't going to waste my energy. I swiped my damp cheeks. Damn the man!

I gave in to the torrent...

The phone rang.

I lifted my head, listening to the peals with a dull sort of recognition. I would have jumped to my feet if I hadn't felt as if a twenty-ton truck had backed over me. I swung my legs off the bed, moving slowly with the foggy pressure in my head.

I was in no hurry. It wasn't likely Rick would come out to answer it—he hadn't had any calls since he'd arrived.

I lifted the phone.

'Hey, Casey,' Sophie lilted melodiously.

'Sophie, you have the most perfect timing. I want to tell you—' But the words clogged in my throat. I couldn't tell her just yet what a fool I was. It was bad enough to have fallen for a married man—it wasn't as if I'd expected a future with him—but to fall for a lying jerk, that was a whole different tragedy. 'It's so good to hear your voice.'

'Thanks, honey.'

'I guess you're ringing to see how the date went with Anthony,' I said flatly. 'It could have gone better.'

'I heard. He called. He said the man you're sharing your place with not only warned him off but set a snake on him. Is that true?'

Rick had warned him off? My chest warmed. Did I mean something to him more than just a convenient place to keep an eye on Courtney?

The hairs on the back of my neck rippled to attention. I turned slowly. Rick stood in the shadows by the front door, his jacket on, covering his

T-shirt, wearing his usual blue jeans and with several bags by his feet.

I'd wanted to be rid of him for so long, but now—now the thought of him leaving was splintering my heart into hot, jagged shards.

'Rick…' His name escaped my lips like a sigh.

He shoved his hands in his pockets, staring at me as though he was memorising every inch of me. 'Casey.' His voice was deep and husky. 'I'll get going now.'

I bit my lip, lowering the phone into the cradle. 'Not without answering some of my questions.'

He crossed his arms over his chest. 'Like what?'

I had no idea. I just wanted it to be right. I urged my brain to brilliance. 'Like how can you leave with that guy still on the loose?'

'He's been caught. My mate—her ex—just called.' He waved a mobile phone in his hand, then slipped it onto his belt. 'He was caught in Colac, heading west.'

'Oh.' I wiped my trembling hands down my trousers, and swallowed. 'Why did you have to lie to me?'

'Would you have let me stay if I'd told you the truth?' His voice wavered.

I stared at my bare feet. Of course I wouldn't have. I was firmly fixed on being alone. I was happy being alone. And work had been enough for me. Sort of. Until he'd walked into my life…

I couldn't ignore the wrenching ache in my chest, or the fact that there was something about Rick that was different. What I felt for him, what he made me feel, was more solid and real than so much of my life it scared me.

I loved him. I truly, madly, deeply loved him, with all my heart. And until now I hadn't realised. I'd never had anything like this before—not even with Alex. This was *real love*, and I owed it to myself to find out if *I* meant anything to *him* at all.

I moved towards him slowly. 'That was Anthony on the phone. He wants another date,' I lied shamelessly. If there was any hope…

'I wish you all the best, Casey. And every happiness.' His gaze dropped to my feet. 'He's obviously a man more worthy of you than I thought.'

My chest warmed. 'You said he wasn't my type. What do you think my type is?'

'It's not important.'

I walked slowly to him and looked up into his handsome face. I couldn't miss the pain etched into the grim lines.

'Haven't you got anything you want to say to me?' I crossed my fingers and prayed.

'I have just three small words for you.' He sucked in his chest and stared into my eyes with an intensity that should have scared me.

I held my breath. My mind grappled to predict what the three words were going to be. *I'm leaving now* or *Goodbye, then, Casey*.

He dragged me closer, pinning me by the shoulders with his strong hands, and looking down at me with those deep blue eyes that I'd never see again.

'I love you.'

My breath caught in my throat. I so wanted it to be true, but I couldn't pretend any more. I couldn't live on delusions. 'You can't love me. You don't even know me.' I bit my lip, staring up into his face.

I could see the truth written plainly in his eyes. He knew me. He knew me too well. There was no hiding from him. He knew I hated cleaning, avoided cooking, had unusual pets, ate chocolate-chip ice cream, and that I looked like a walking bird's nest in the morning.

His grip softened, his thumbs rubbing my skin with a gentleness that sent aches careering through my body. His lips caught mine and all thought was dashed by the waves of desire he was evoking.

I closed my eyes and lived the moment, savouring his touch, the soft gentleness of his lips against mine, his scent and his taste. And I yearned. I yearned for him to be Mr Right when all logic was telling me he was wrong.

I stepped back, wrapping my arms around myself. 'And I don't know you. You're a stranger to me.'

'A stranger is just a friend you haven't met yet,' Rick said, his voice velvet-soft. 'My name's Eric Harrison. Pleased to meet you.' He held out his hand to me.

I looked at his large square hand dubiously. *His name wasn't even Rick.* My mind staggered. Could I take the risk of him dashing my heart into pieces? But then, my heart was a mess already. Could the wrong guy be the right guy?

'I don't trust you,' I admitted, looking at his chest instead of his hand, the words fighting with the feelings raging deep within me.

'You don't trust any male.'

'I trust George.' I bit my lip. I knew what he'd say next. That George was just a dog. That he didn't count.

He smiled. 'Well, George trusts me. Animals can tell if a person's okay,' Eric said softly, still holding his hand towards me. 'You can trust me too, Casey.'

Warm tingles raced down my spine and into the pit of my stomach. I couldn't ignore my heart any longer. I put my hand in his big, warm, strong one and held on tight. I took a deep, steadying breath. 'And what do you do for work, Mr Harrison?'

'Call me Eric. I used to be a cop. Now I run my own business.' His grip on my hand tightened and he pulled me closer. 'Will you give me a second chance?' he asked, his velvet-soft voice washing over me.

I looked up into his beautiful blue eyes and smiled.

There was so much I didn't know about Eric... And, curiosity being my curse, I couldn't resist...